Dani Collins

Vows of Revenge

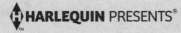

HARLEQUIN PRESENTS®

Recycling programs
for this product may
not exist in your area.

ISBN-13: 978-0-373-13373-4

Vows of Revenge

First North American Publication 2015

Copyright © 2015 by Dani Collins

Printed in U.S.A.

Vows of Revenge

In my heart, my books are always dedicated to my husband and kids, my sisters and my parents. They've always been incredibly supportive, both emotionally and by physically doing dishes and making meals so I could write.

When it comes to writing dedications, however, I often look to my editors. Writing is a lonely business. I'm a big enough control freak that I don't ask other writers to look at my work and weigh in. It's all on me until I hit Send. Then I rely on my editor to ensure I'm not embarrassing myself.

Kathryn Cheshire is my latest wing-woman in the Harlequin Mills & Boon® offices. This is our first book together and she's everything an author wants and needs: warm, insightful and encouraging.

I couldn't do this without my family or you, Dear Reader, but a great editor is the linchpin in the whole operation. Thanks for being awesome, Kathryn.

"What do you really want from me, Melodie?" Roman asked in his deadliest tone, willing her to come clean.

"Just, um... Honestly?" She blinked up at him, practically virginal with her gaze damp and defenseless, her mouth working to find words. "For you to kiss me again," she said, voice a thin husk. "To see if..." She licked her lips, leaving an expectant silence.

"Come and get it, then," he said gruffly, trying to scoff, telling himself he was only seeing the extent she'd go in this industrial espionage of hers, letting her demean herself when he had every intention of rejecting her.

But it didn't happen that way.

She absorbed his command with a small flinch, then lifted her chin as though gathering her courage. As she stepped up to him, her hands opened on his rib cage in a feathery tickle that made his entire body jerk in reaction. She was tall enough that when she lifted on tiptoes, her mouth reached his.

She pressed pillowy lips to his. He told himself to shove her back and tell her—

The rocking of her mouth beneath his parted his lips. He closed his arms around her, pulled her into him with a strength he barely remembered to temper and slanted his mouth to take full possession of hers.

She opened to him, arched and pressed into him and moaned capitulation.

Rational thought evaporated in a groan of craving.

Canadian **Dani Collins** knew in high school that she wanted to write romance for a living. Twenty-five years later, after marrying her high school sweetheart, having two kids with him, working several generic office jobs and submitting countless manuscripts, she got "The Call." Her first Harlequin Presents romance novel won the Reviewers' Choice Award for Best First in Series from *RT Book Reviews*. She now works in her own office, writing romance.

Books by Dani Collins

Harlequin Presents

Seduced into the Greek's World
The Russian's Acquisition
An Heir to Bind Them
A Debt Paid in Passion
More than a Convenient Marriage?
No Longer Forbidden?

Seven Sexy Sins

The Sheikh's Sinful Seduction

The 21st Century Gentleman's Club

The Ultimate Seduction

One Night With Consequences

Proof of Their Sin

Visit the Author Profile page
at Harlequin.com for more titles.

CHAPTER ONE

SURROUNDED BY OLD money and cold-blooded cynicism for the first part of her life, Melodie Parnell wasn't half as ingenuous as she looked. In fact, she actively tried to give off an air of sophistication by straightening her curly brown hair into a shiny curtain, adding a flick of liquid liner to downplay her round blue eyes and painting a bold red lipstick over her plump, pink lips. Her clothing choices were classic business style: a pencil skirt, a sweater set and her mother's pearls.

At the same time, she privately offered people the benefit of the doubt. She believed the best whenever possible and always sought the brightest side of every situation.

That attitude had earned her nothing but contempt from her half brother and more than once resulted in a sting from social climbers and gold diggers trying to get closer to the men in her family. Being softhearted had definitely been her mother's downfall. But, Melodie often assured herself, she wasn't nearly as fragile or susceptible as that. The fact that she'd lost her mother very recently and kept slipping into a state of melancholy as she faced life without her didn't make her vulnerable.

Yet, for some reason, Roman Killian took the rug right out from under her—by doing nothing except answering the door of his mansion.

"You must be the indispensable Melodie," he greeted.

She was supposed to be immune to powerful men in

bespoke outfits, but her mouth went dry and her knees
went weak. He wasn't even wearing a suit. He wore a casually tailored linen jacket over black pants and a collar-
less peasant-style shirt, three open buttons at his throat.

Not that she really took in his clothes. She saw the man.

He had black hair that might have curled if he let it
grow long enough, tanned skin and gorgeous bone struc-
ture. Italian? Spanish? Greek? He certainly had the refined
features of European aristocracy, but Melodie knew him
to be a self-made American. His brows were straight and
circumspect, his eyes decidedly green with a dark ring
around the irises. He was clean shaven, urbane and acutely
masculine in every way.

He met her gaze with an impactful directness that stole
her breath.

"Roman Killian," he said, offering his hand and snapping her out of her fixation. His voice was like dark choc-
olate and red wine, rich and sultry, but his tone held a hint
of disparagement. No one was truly essential, he seemed
to say.

"I am Melodie," she managed to say. She watched his
mouth as he clasped her hand in his strong grip. His upper
lip was much narrower than his full bottom one. He smiled
in the way men did when confronted with a woman they
didn't find particularly attractive, but were forced by circumstance to be polite toward. Cool and dismissive.

Melodie wasn't offended. She was always braced for
male rejection and surprised if she didn't get it. It wasn't
that she was homely. She had just inherited her mother's
catwalk build and elfin features along with her pearls. The
attributes were fine for modeling, but came off as skinny
and exaggerated in real life. Spiderlike and awkward—
or so she'd been told so many times she tended to believe
it.

So his indifference wasn't a surprise, but her skin still

prickled and she warmed as though the sun had lodged in her belly and radiated outward through her limbs with a disarming feeling that she was glowing.

She shouldn't be so nervous. She'd still had a pacifier in her mouth when she'd begun glad-handing, and rarely suffered shyness no matter how lofty the person she was meeting. Presidents. Royalty. Such things didn't affect her.

Yet she found herself surreptitiously fighting to catch her breath, aware that she was letting her hand stay in his too long. When she tried to extract it, however, he tightened his grip.

"We've met," he said with certainty. Almost accusingly. His eyes narrowed as he raked her face with his gaze, head cocked and arrested.

"No," she assured him, but her pulse gave a leap while a romantic part of her brain invented a fanciful "in another life soul-mate" scenario. She was very good with faces and names, though, even when a person wasn't nearly as memorable as he was. And he was too young to remember her mother, not that he looked the type to thumb through fashion magazines in the first place. There was an off chance he'd seen her in connection to her father, she supposed, but she was carving that particular man from her life one thought at a time so she didn't bring him up, and only said, "I'm quite sure we haven't."

Roman didn't believe her, she could see it.

"Ingrid and Huxley aren't with you?" He flicked a look for her clients to where her taxi had dropped her next to the fountain in his paved courtyard.

"They'll be along shortly," she said.

He brought his sharp gaze back to her face, making her quiver inwardly again. Slowly he released her and waved toward the interior of his home. "Come in."

"Thank you," she murmured, disconcerted by everything about him.

He was so masculine, so confident yet aloof. Secure, she thought, with a twist of irony. He'd made his fortune in security, starting with a software package but now offering global solutions of all kinds. It was one of the few things she knew about him. She hadn't researched him much, mostly relying on what Ingrid had shared, turned off by the idea she might wind up reading about her half brother if she looked up Roman online.

But knowing he was Anton's competition *had* made her predisposed to like Roman. He also seemed to have a streak of magnanimity, supporting causes from homelessness to dementia research to donating computers to libraries. And he'd offered his home in the south of France for his employee's wedding. Surely that meant he possessed a big heart under that air of predatory power?

"I didn't expect a security specialist to have such a welcoming home," she confessed, trying to ignore the sense that his eyes stayed glued to her narrow shoulders as she took in a modern house built with old-world grandeur. "I imagined something very contemporary, made of glass and stainless steel, all sharp angles."

The high ceilings held glittering chandeliers. A double staircase came down in expansive arms of delicate wrought iron and sumptuous red carpet over yellowed marble. The tiles continued through the huge foyer to an enormous lounge where a horseshoe sofa in warm terra-cotta would easily seat twenty.

Did he entertain often? Something in the way his energy permeated this airy interior so thoroughly made her think he kept this all-comfortable splendor to himself.

"The sorts of things that people want to protect are often attractive. Jewelry. Art," he supplied with a negligent shrug. "Six inches of steel works to a point, but surveillance and alarms allow for designs that are more aesthetically pleasing."

"Are we being filmed right now?" she asked with a lilt of surprise.

"The cameras are only activated when an alarm is tripped."

So it was just him was watching her, then. Nerve-racking all the same.

A formal dining room stood off to the right. It could be useful for the waitstaff, perhaps, since the four hundred wedding guests would eat in tents outside. And yes, the property allowed plenty of room for the ceremony, tents, a bandstand and a dance floor. Arched breezeways lined the house where it faced the Mediterranean. In the court-yard stood a square pool with a quarter circle taken out of it like a bite for a small dining area. Beyond its turquoise water a half dozen stairs led to a long strip of sandy beach. Off to the right a tethered helicopter stood on a groomed lawn. Once it had been removed, that space would be per-fect for the ceremony and reception.

Melodie had grown up in luxury, but nothing as ex-travagant as this. Roman Killian was a very rich man. It was difficult to hide how awed she was.

She brought her gaze back to the bougainvillea train-ing up the colonnades, and smaller pots of roses and ge-raniums and flowers she couldn't identify. They gave off scents of anise and cherry and honey, dreamy and adding to the magical atmosphere of the place.

"This is all so beautiful," she murmured, trying not to see herself as a bride, spilling in a waterfall of white lace down the stairs, emerging to blinding light and a strikingly handsome groom. The sunset would paint their future in rosy pink. Candlelight would burn like their eternal love.

She met Roman's gaze and found him eyeing her as if reading her thoughts, making her blush and look away.

"It's very generous of you to offer it," she managed.

"Ingrid is an exceptional employee," he said after a brief

pause, making her think that wasn't his real reason for offering his home. "Why didn't you all come together? Are
you not staying at the same hotel?"

"They're newly engaged," Melodie said wryly. "I've
been feeling very third wheel since meeting them at the
airport." It was only four days, she reminded herself.

"Job hazard?" Roman guessed with a twitch around
his mouth.

She couched a smile, suspecting he had a much lower
tolerance than she did for witnessing nuzzling and baby
talk.

"It can be," she replied, aiming for circumspect, because this was only her second wedding and her first international society one. Her business was still so new the
price tag hadn't been clipped off, but he didn't need to
know that. She'd organized state dinners in her sleep, and
this was exactly the sort of event she was ready to build
her livelihood upon.

"How long have you been living here?" She was highly
curious about him.

His manner changed. Their moment of commonality
evaporated and she had the impression he stepped back
from his body, leaving only the shell before her.

"It was completed last year. What else can I show you?
The kitchen?"

"Thank you," she said, hiding her surprise at how
quickly she'd been shut down.

He waved her toward the end of the house, where he
introduced her to his personal chef. The Frenchman was
standoffish but had nothing on his employer. She was able
to get a few details about the catering cleared up as Roman
stood watch, keeping her on high alert.

Roman expected the single pulse from his silenced watch
to be a notification that the rest of his guests had arrived.

One glance at the face told him it was actually a request that he review an important security alert.

Given that security was his business, he didn't take the request lightly, but an immediate threat would have been flagged as such and dealt with at the perimeter. And he had a guest. This wisp of a woman flickering through his home like sunlight and shadow through a copse of trees fascinated him. The conviction that she was familiar was incredibly strong, yet he'd sensed no lie when she'd assured him they were strangers.

Roman had a reliable radar for lies, one he listened to without fail. The one time he'd ignored his gut and convinced himself to have faith, he'd lost everything up to, and almost including, his life.

So even though he should have forced himself to the panel on the wall to review the alert, he stayed with his PA's wedding planner, keeping her under observation—partly, he admitted to himself, because her backside was delightfully outlined by her snug skirt, proving she was round and perky in the right places. He liked listening to her voice, too. Her accent wasn't heavy like Americans from the Deep South, but it had a lick of molasses, sweet and slow with a hint of rough darkness as she elevated and dropped each word. Very engaging.

She puzzled him at the same time. He was used to women being overt when they were attracted to him. He wasn't so arrogant he thought all of them were, but he worked out, wore tailored clothes and was loaded. These were all things that typically appealed to the opposite sex. She was blushing and flicking him nervous looks, fiddling with her hair, obviously very aware of him, but trying to hide it.

She wasn't wearing a ring, but perhaps she was involved with someone. If she wasn't, that shyness suggested she preferred slow, complex relationships. She didn't sleep with men for the fun of it, he surmised, which was a pity because that was very much a quality he looked for in a woman.

Roman had trained himself to keep emotions firmly at bay, but a blanket of disappointment descended on him. He was attracted to her, but apparently it wouldn't go anywhere. That was a shame.

Melodie had noticed his glance at his watch and offered a wry smile. "Perhaps I shouldn't have left the happy couple to their own devices. They're quite late, aren't they?"

"It's not like Ingrid," he allowed. If it had been, she wouldn't be his PA. He wasn't a tyrant, but he didn't tolerate sloppy behavior of any kind.

At the same time, he was fine with having Melodie to himself for a little longer.

"Perhaps you could show me where she'll dress?" she suggested, and showed him her smartphone. "I wouldn't mind taking note of suitable photo locations. The bridal preparations and procession to the groom are always an important part of the day's record."

"Are they?" If he sounded disdainful, he couldn't help it. He had lived hand to mouth for long enough that he didn't see the point in extravagant ceremonies. Did he pay for top quality now that he could afford to? Absolutely. But weddings were already given too much importance without turning them into a Broadway musical—then filming behind-the-scenes footage for others to ooh and aah over. As much as he appreciated Ingrid for all the skills she brought to her work, he was hosting this performance strictly for business reasons.

"I take it you're not a romantic," Melodie said as though reading his cynicism. "Or is it just that you wish you hadn't agreed to having your private space invaded?"

Both, he admitted silently, and realized he would have

to work on controlling how much he revealed around this woman. She was very astute.

Or very attuned to him, which was even more disturbing.

"I'm a dedicated realist," he replied, motioning for her to lead the way from the kitchen up a flight of service stairs to a breakfast room. "You?" he drawled.

"Hopeless optimist," she confessed without apology. "Oh, this room is gorgeous."

It was the second time she'd forced him to take stock of the choices he'd made in his surroundings. Part of him had been willing to go with the sort of design she'd said she expected of him: glass and chrome and clean, straight lines. But he'd spent enough time in an institution—juvenile, so not quite as stark as real prison—along with houses that weren't his own. He'd wanted something that felt like a real home. Of course, it also had to be a smart investment that would fetch a tidy profit if his world ever collapsed again and he had to sell it. Which wouldn't happen, but Roman was a plan B and C and D sort of man.

So even though he ate in this sunroom every morning, he wasn't as charmed as she appeared to be by its earthy tones and view overlooking the lemon groves between the road and the fountain in front of the house. He had agreed with the architect that having the morning sunlight pour in through the windows made sense, as did the French doors that opened to the upper balcony that ran the side and length of the house facing the pool and the sea, but it could rain every morning for all the notice he took.

"I once had a fortune cookie that told me to always be optimistic because nothing else matters."

Her remark caught him by surprise. His mouth twitched as he processed the irony. He quickly controlled it, but couldn't help bantering, "They should all read, 'You're about to eat a dry, tasteless cracker.'"

"Ouch." She mock frowned at him. "I dread to ask what you think of weddings if that's your attitude toward fortune cookies. Dry and tasteless?" she surmised with a blink of her wide eyes.

She was definitely flirting with him.

Time to let her know that if she went down that road it would be for short-term amusement, not long-term commitment.

"The ceremony does strike me as a rather elaborate shell for a piece of paper that promises something about the future but ultimately has no bearing on what will really happen."

His denunciation had her shoulders dropping in dismay. "That would be poetic if it wasn't so depressing," she informed him. "Weddings are as much a celebration of the happiness that has been achieved thus far as they are a promise of happily-ever-after."

"You promise that, do you? Sounds as if you're taking advantage of the gullible."

"Meaning that people who fall in love and make plans to share their lives are suckers? On the contrary—they haven't given up hope," she defended, lifting her chin with pretended insult.

"For?" he challenged, secretly enjoying this lighthearted battle of opinion.

"Whatever it is they seek. How far would you have come with your company if you hadn't dreamed beyond what looked realistic? If all you'd done was aim low?" She gave him a cheeky smile as she walked past him into his private sitting room, meeting his eyes as though sure she had him. "See? Being an optimist, I believe I can convert you."

"I'm not that easy to manipulate," he stated, confident he'd maintained the upper hand. "But go ahead and try," he added with significance.

CHAPTER TWO

"OKAY— OH." THE sitting room took up the corner of the house facing the water. More French doors opened to both the side and front balcony. The rest of the area was clearly the master bedroom.

Melodie had been so caught up in trying to be clever she hadn't realized where she was going. She blushed. "I didn't realize." Why hadn't he stopped her?

"There's a guest room down the hall that Ingrid can use to dress," he said drily.

She should have hurried to find it, but her feet fixed to the carpet as she took in the luxurious room in varying shades of blue. The bed was obscenely huge and was backed by mirrors to reflect the view. The wall onto the balcony was made of glass doors that doubled back on themselves so many times they ended up tucked into the corners. The partition between outside and interior had essentially disappeared.

Filmy curtains hung in tied bunches at the corners of the bed, presumably to afford some privacy to the occupant— occupants, plural?—if they happened to be in the bed with the doors open.

With that thought Melodie became acutely aware of the fact that she was a woman and Roman a man. He was tall and broad and his bed would accommodate his strapping body easily, along with any company he brought with him. She swallowed, trying not to betray the direction her thoughts were taking, even as she felt heat creeping through her, staining her cheeks.

As far as what he might be thinking, it was hard to tell whether he was attracted to her or just amusing himself at her expense.

"Oh, that's very beautiful," she said, letting the view draw her onto the balcony and away from the intimacy of his bedroom. She set her purse near her feet and used two hands to steady her phone while she took a snap. Her faint trembles grew worse as Roman came to stand next to her.

"How do you know Ingrid?" he asked.

Uncomfortable remaining where she could smell the traces of his aftershave, Melodie moved along the upper balcony, trying to pretend her dazzled state was caused by the band of turquoise just beyond the white beach before the blue of the sea deepened to navy. An indolent breeze moved through her sweater and hair, doing little to cool her. It was more of a disturbing caress, really. Inciting.

"Our mothers went to the same prep school in Virginia." Looking for cool in the wrought iron rail, Melodie grasped only heat, but she let the hard cut of metal into her palm ground her as she added, "My mother passed away recently and Evelyn came to the service. It was auspicious timing, with Ingrid recently becoming engaged."

Melodie's father had been instrumental in this new job of hers, of course, not that she intended to broadcast that. After insisting they invite Evelyn to say a few words about Melodie's mother—a request that had surprised the woman when she hadn't spoken to her old friend in years—Garner had insisted Melodie go talk to her. Ask her about her daughter. Melodie had realized after the fact that Garner had been fishing for info on Roman through his PA, but she didn't know why. She'd taken her time following up with Evelyn a couple of weeks after the service and kept it to herself. Her father and brother didn't even know she was here. Heck, they didn't know she was alive. She preferred it that way.

"Helping with the arrangements has taken my mind off things," she provided with a faint smile. "Weddings are such happy occasions. Far better than organizing a funeral."

A pause, then he asked, perplexed, "Are you saying the funeral was so impressive it prompted this woman to ask you to arrange her daughter's wedding?"

Melodie chuckled, even though the subject was still very raw for her.

"Not exactly. It *was* a grand affair," she allowed, trying to keep the disdain out of her voice. Her mother had wanted something small and private. Her father had wanted publicity shots. Melodie had wanted her mother's ashes. She'd done what she had to and the urn was now in her home, where she'd keep it safe until she could complete her mother's final wish, to have her ashes scattered in Paris. "But I think Evelyn was being kind to me, suggesting I get into this sort of thing as a career—"

Oops. She hadn't meant to reveal that. Shooting a glance at Roman, she saw his brows had gone up with that detail.

"Which isn't to say I'm not qualified," she hurried to assure him. This wouldn't be amateur hour with monkeys stumbling around his home overturning his life, if that was what he was thinking behind that analytical expression. Melodie intended to repay Evelyn's faith in her by ensuring each detail of her daughter's wedding went off perfectly and with the utmost taste. "I've done a lot of this type of thing, just hadn't seen it as a career possibility. After she said what she did, I contacted her and we came to an arrangement."

"So you're just getting your company off the ground. There must be substantial investment up front," he commented. "Flying here to scout the location. That sort of thing."

"Some," she replied with suitable vagueness. Complaining about money problems would not inspire his confidence. But the small policy she'd managed to take out on her mother's behalf had merely paid for the worst of her health-care bills. Pretending she could afford a weekend in the south of France was pure bravado and something Melodie would build into Ingrid and Huxley's final bill.

"Your office," she assumed as she moved away from that topic and along the balcony, arriving in front of a pair of open doors. The interior of the room held a desk free of clutter surrounded by large, clear screens she previously had thought were an invention confined to sci-fi movies. "You'll want to secure this on the day, obviously."

A door led off one wall back into his bedroom. The opposite wall was completely covered in large flat screens. A single image of his company logo took up the black space on them.

Melodie stepped into the room, drawn by its spare yet complex setup. A blip sounded and Roman followed to press his thumb pad to a sensor.

"You're quite the secret agent, aren't you?" she teased.

"I like to consider myself the man who stops them," he rejoined drily.

She bit back a smile at his supreme confidence and said, "This would be a stunning angle for a photo, with the water in the background. Would you stand in for Ingrid?"

"Not likely," he dismissed. Then smoothly turned things around with "You'd make a prettier bride. I'll take the photo." He held out his hand for her phone.

She hesitated, far more comfortable behind the lens than in front of it. She always had been, but she really didn't want to cause even the smallest ripple in such a big commission.

"If you prefer," she murmured with false equanimity and readied her camera app, walking back outside again as she did so. "We'll do a series of shots from when the father of the bride fetches her from her room and all the way down the stairs. I had thought she'd come down the interior ones, but these ones are better. The guests will see her approach, and all this wrought iron is so gorgeous. We'll take some couple shots on the inside stairs after the ceremony." She was thinking aloud as she went to the rail and turned to face him.

He fiddled with her phone, then said, "Ready."

After a few of the app's manufactured clicks, he lifted his gaze and commanded, "Smile. You're getting married."

Caught off guard, Melodie laughed with natural humor, then clasped an imaginary bouquet and channeled her best bridal joy, as if the man of her dreams was awaiting her.

Despite being mocked mercilessly through her teens and suffering a self-imposed disaster that had put her off dating into her adult years, she had been telling the truth about being a romantic. She liked to believe a real-life hero existed for her. She *needed* to believe it, or she'd become as depressed as her mother had been.

Her mother's illness had held Melodie back from looking for him, but now, despite the grief abrading her heart, she was open to possibility. Willing to take a risk. For just this one moment she let herself imagine *Roman* was the man made for her. Her soul mate.

Roman's intense concentration lifted sharply from the phone, pinning her in the steely needle of his hard stare.

"What's wrong?" she asked. Heat climbed up her chest into her throat.

"Nothing."

She licked her lips and moved along the balcony toward the outer stairs, trying to escape the moment of silly make-believe, but now that it was in her head she couldn't help wondering what it would be like to live with this savagely beautiful man.

Hard, she thought. *But the right woman might be able to soften him.*

The stairs descended in a curve to the area beside the pool. She stopped at the top and waved behind herself.

"She'll have a train. We'll fan it out here." She twisted as she indicated the puddle of imaginary silk and lace. Lifting her gaze, looking back over her shoulder at him as if this was a bad idea. She was too far into the dream, unguarded and vulnerable. She had accidentally left herself open to his reading her thoughts. Her entire body became paralyzed in a kind of thrilled panic, as though he'd happened upon her naked, but she wasn't afraid or ashamed. She was a nymph caught by a god.

He went statue still.

Her phone looked small in his hand, clicking, but practically forgotten as he looked past it and kept his eyes on her, taking his time as he toured her shoulder blades and waist and bottom and legs. The term *brutally handsome* came into her head and she understood it for the first time in her life. Roman was so gorgeous it was an assault to the senses, squeezing her lungs and pulsing heat under her skin.

He frightened her, but she wanted him to pursue her. It didn't make sense, but from everything she'd heard about hormones, they were never big on logic. They were the opposite, and hers were responding unusually well to him. *That* was what frightened her. Not him, per se, but her reaction to him.

He abruptly glanced at his watch. "Ingrid has been delayed," he said, touching the device. "She thinks she sprained her wrist. She's at the clinic and asks if we can reschedule."

* * *

He could have asked Melodie to stay for lunch, but he didn't. He had his driver take her back to her hotel. He wanted time to consider how he was reacting to her before pursuing her openly.

Powerfully was the answer to how he was reacting. Taking her photo had been an excuse to study her, and he hadn't seen a single thing he didn't like. And even though he was far beyond getting hot over photos of women, clothed or not, for some reason he'd been fixated as he had watched her pose. There was definitely a strong sexual attraction between them, but more than that, he'd found her magnetic.

Why?

He shook off his perplexity as he pressed his thumb pad to the sensor in his office and tapped the screen, bringing up the security report he'd ignored earlier.

He swore aloud as the contents became clear.

Apparently the experts were right. He was a security genius, if late to the party this once. The myriad details that his gatekeeper and even his own eyes had missed had been refined by his closed circuit camera and proprietary software, filtered against online content, then tagged to warn him of an attack even more insidious than the one he'd suffered all those years ago.

A handful of matches had come up. He glanced through them, stomach knotting.

The surname comparison could be dismissed as coincidental. Melodie had given his guard the name Parnell, which had been tagged to Parnell-Gautier. Two and a half decades ago, a model named Patience Parnell had hyphenated to Parnell-Gautier when she married.

He flicked to a dated glamor shot from a defunct fashion magazine. Patience stared at him, young and nubile, her gamine face bearing a striking resemblance to Melodie's big eyes and wide mouth. And there she was holding a baby girl named Charmaine. Not Melodie, but the date would put the baby in her early twenties today, precisely the age Melodie appeared to be.

Roman had met Patience once, very briefly, he recalled now. But he'd never considered her a direct threat because she'd gone into some kind of medical care several years ago.

His war, Roman had always believed, was with Anton Gautier and Anton's father, Garner Gautier. Aside from one recent photograph, the daughter hadn't been linked publically to either man since childhood.

He studied the photograph from a newsfeed dated two months ago. Melodie's profile from her approach in the taxi today had been set against the profile in the news piece where a backlit woman, wearing a black hat with a netted veil, stood next to her American senator father as he bowed his head over a casket. Behind them stood Anton. The caption mentioned that Patience Parnell-Gautier was survived by her loving husband, stepson and daughter, Charmaine *M.* Parnell-Gautier.

How vile and just like Gautier to send his second spawn into Roman's house like this. To use his PA's *mother* to infiltrate his home.

He immediately dismissed any thought that Ingrid could be in on the scheme. She'd proved her loyalty again and again over the years. And it had been his idea to host the wedding, not hers. High-society circles were small and tight. She had connections he didn't. He wouldn't care about being accepted at that level if it weren't for the fact that it was the one area the Gautiers had an advantage on him. He'd volunteered his home to even the playing field.

What he couldn't understand was how Melodie had captivated him to the point that he'd ignored the security alert rather than read it and order her off his property. He wasn't so uncivilized he'd have had her *thrown* out the way he'd been physically expelled from her father's campaign office twelve years ago. Battered and kicked so badly he could barely walk away. Anton had been the thief, but Garner had had the power to turn it around and call Roman the criminal. He'd had the power to ruin Roman, which he had.

A red haze of fury rose with the recollection. He would *not* allow the Gautiers to play him again. Rage urged him to hurt them, deeply, for daring to try.

Despite being a man who actively sublimated everything resembling feelings, he found himself able to taste delicious vengeance on the tip of his tongue. He'd been longing to get back at this family for years, biding his time, wanting to first overtake Gautier Enterprises in the arena that would cause them the most discomfort: financial.

For years, their two companies had been neck and neck in a two-horse race, both improving on the same software that he, Roman, originally had written and that Anton had convinced him his father would back. Instead, the men had stolen his product, finished it, then made a mint while Roman had scraped by for another five years, rebuilding everything he'd lost and finally entering the marketplace so far behind them he'd despaired of ever catching up.

Finally, early last year, he had begun to see parity. It wasn't enough. Not for him. He'd risked everything and had thrown all his resources behind completely reengineered software. The gamble had paid off. Corporations were dropping the dated Gautier knockoff and stampeding to Roman's new, far superior product.

Gautier's bottom line had to be feeling the pinch by now. It followed that they would send in a scout, thinking to once again steal what they wanted and step back into the top position.

Like *hell*.

Roman wasn't just going to win this time. He would

send a message to the Gautiers they would never forget. He would crush them into nothing, starting by flattening their emissary without a shred of mercy.

His first instinct was to have Ingrid fire Melodie immediately, but he forced himself to more coolheaded contemplation. The Gautiers had let Roman believe he was on the path to success right up to the moment when they explained his services with the software design were no longer needed and they would be taking possession of his ticket to a better life.

Therefore, he would ensure he had another wedding planner in place, so there was no inconvenience to Ingrid. Melodie would lose her contract and any chance of continuing in that field. Nice of her to drop the detail that it was a new venture, he reflected. He didn't think for a moment she was serious about making a career of wedding planning, but as with any con artist's ruse, the Gautiers would have put funds behind making it seem real. He was glad to at least cost them their investment.

A few investigative keystrokes later, he saw that Melodie lived alone. Surprisingly modestly, he noted. So had he, back in the day, but he'd still lost his home and all he owned. He knew that his eye-for-an-eye retribution wouldn't have the same impact. Melodie would simply run home to Daddy, but it was the right message, so he started the wheels rolling on getting her kicked out.

The final touch would be the simple, crystal clear message that they'd failed. The sweetest retaliation of all.

Melodie had clearly pulled the rookie move of plugging her phone into the charger without checking that it was properly connected. When she pulled it off, one foot out the door to meet Ingrid and Huxley and leave for Roman's, she saw it had not only failed to charge, but had lost the 4 percent it had had. Dead as a doornail.

Sparing a moment to throw it into the safe with her passport, she wound up putting her whole purse inside. She'd take a credit card as a just-in-case, but it was only going to be a quick lunch in a private home. She didn't need to pack a bag.

Okay, yes, her mind was racing a mile a minute and she couldn't make a rational decision to save her life. She was not just nervous but excited. Last night with Ingrid and Huxley it had been all she could do to keep her chatter confined to the suitability of Roman's house as a venue for the wedding. The whole time she'd been longing to pump her client for more information on Roman, but she'd managed to wait until bed before doing a bit more online snooping. Then she'd lain awake fantasizing about him—creating scenarios in her head she hadn't ever starred in before, but wanted to with him.

A short while later, having met up with Ingrid and Huxley en route, Melodie barely kept herself from dancing in place as Roman opened his door to them.

"I'm so *sorry*," Ingrid moaned as they entered. "I slipped in the tub the other night and didn't think it was that bad, but by the time we were on our way here yesterday, it was like this." She motioned a ballooned wrist.

"She wanted to wait until we'd finished here before going to the clinic, but she was fighting tears in the car," Huxley said. "I couldn't let it go untreated."

"Of course not," Roman murmured smoothly. "I'm glad it's just a sprain, and won't impact your typing and filing once your vacation is finished."

Ingrid giggled. "He's being funny," she said to Melodie over her shoulder. "The office is paperless and we do almost everything talk to text."

Melodie smiled, wishing that Ingrid and Huxley weren't pressed to each other like a pair of bubbles that were about to become one. She really needed them to diffuse all this aggressive male energy coming her way. It was as if Roman had developed a ten-fold power of masculinity overnight and it was now all beamed directly at her.

"Excellent photos, by the way. You have a hidden talent," Ingrid said to her boss, thankfully drawing his attention for a brief moment.

He only said, "The camera loves her," then trained his intent gaze back onto Melodie as though searching for something.

Huxley wanted to know what they were talking about and Melodie immediately regretted showing the photos to Ingrid. She'd been trying to explain the potential for wedding photos, but now had to brush aside Ingrid's gushing with a brisk "I was hamming."

The final shot, where she'd been looking back at Roman, was the most disturbing. Her slender figure against the ivory backdrop of the mansion's west wing had projected elegant femininity while her expression had been one of sensual invitation. She hadn't meant to be so…revealing.

Embarrassment struck once again as yesterday's unfounded yearnings welled anew. This was why she hated having her picture taken. Too much of herself became visible.

"Why don't we go outside and you can take a few photos yourself?" she suggested, trying to distract everyone.

As they sat down by the poolside for a light lunch, Roman continued to study Melodie, biding his time, confident yet highly cautious. She was a surprisingly dangerous woman beneath that projected innocence.

He'd thought her pretty yesterday, which had apparently been enough to mesmerize him. Today, having seen the glimpse of unfettered beauty in her photos, he now caught flashes of stunning attractiveness in her as she smiled and exchanged banter with Ingrid and Huxley.

The truth was he was having trouble remembering why he shouldn't be drawn to her. He told himself he was giving her enough rope to hang herself, but deep down he wondered if he was putting off the denouement of his plan so he could spend a few more minutes admiring her.

It was sick and wrong. She was his enemy. Yet he suddenly found himself ensnared in the meaningful look she was sending him. She practically spoke inside his head as she flicked a rueful glance toward the couple, who had had to take a break from eating to rub noses. *See? It never stops.*

It was an odd moment of being on exactly the same wavelength. An urge to chuckle over their private joke rose in him while the sparkle in her eye and the flash of her smile encouraged him.

What the hell? How could he be gripped by anything except the fact she was here to commit a crime against him?

"Now that you've seen the place, shall I tell my staff it's set in stone?" he asked Ingrid, pulling them all back to the supposed business at hand. Trying to put his train of thought back on its rails.

"Please," Ingrid said, offering him a look of earnest gratitude. "And I can't thank you enough. I'm still reeling that you've been so kind as to offer this. It's his fortress of solitude," she added in a teasing aside to Melodie. "No one is ever invited here."

Roman brushed off the remark with a dry smile, but felt the weight of Melodie's curiosity. He ignored the prickle of male awareness that responded to the intrigue in her gaze, set his inner shields firmly into place and wrote off a trickle of anticipation as a premonition of threat that he would heed.

"We all need a retreat where we can work in peace," he said, partly to tantalize her—*your move*, he was saying—

but his house was more than a sanctuary. It was a statement that he had arrived, and hosting the wedding would
publish that headline.

"Well, it helps a great deal having a central location to
bring the families into, since they're coming from far and
wide," Huxley went on. "We appreciate it."

Roman offered another vague smile, covering up the
fact that he was *very* aware that Huxley's father was a
highly placed British ambassador in the Middle East, and
the rest of his relations were blue bloods from the UK.
Ingrid's were old money Americans, including an aunt
married to a German sitting on the EU Council of Minis-
ters. Ingrid's maid of honor was the daughter of a Swiss
banker. The event was a who's who of the international
renowned and elite.

Being hosted by the son of a New York prostitute.

This was his entrée, he reminded himself dourly, wishing he felt more enthusiasm, but feeling more taken with
the cat-and-mouse game he was playing with Melodie.
What did it say about him that base things such as competition and survival still preoccupied him?

"How did you get into security software development?"
Melodie asked, nearly prompting a sarcastic "really?" out
of him.

He didn't allow himself to be suckered by her solemn
expression of interest. It struck him that she might not be
here to steal, merely to damage. Her family had threatened
to use his background to discredit him once before. They
wouldn't be above trying it again. Perhaps she intended to
sabotage his hosting of the wedding, removing his chance
to grow acquainted with the world's top influencers.

He met her quietly lethal question head-on, neutral-
izing any bombshells she might be poised to detonate by
getting there first.

"I was arrested at fourteen for hacking into a bank's network server."

"Are you serious, Roman?" Ingrid cried on a gasp of intrigue, cutlery rattling onto the edge of her plate. "I had no idea," she exclaimed, eyes wide with delight in the scandal. "You're getting information out of him I never did, Mel!"

Melodie's ridiculously long lashes swept down in a hint of shy pleasure, betraying that she enjoyed the thought of having power over him.

Irritated by the amount of truth in Ingrid's remark— Melodie *was* the reason he was going against habit and bringing up his past—Roman finished the story. If it left this table he was determined it would be framed as closely to the truth as possible, and not twisted to annihilate him the way Melodie's father had threatened.

"Once I realized I could outsmart adults, the game was on to see how far I could go," he said frankly. "The security specialist who caught me, a tough ex-marine named Charles, was impressed, especially because I was self-taught. Once I did my stint in juvenile detention, he brought me onto his payroll. Taught me how to use my talent for good instead of evil," he summed up with mild derision.

Melodie's surprise appeared genuine.

"You weren't expecting honesty?" he challenged.

"It's not that. I've just never met anyone with a natural ability for programming." A shadow flickered behind her eyes, something he barely caught, but it colored her voice as she said, "I thought that sort of thing was a myth."

She was talking about her brother, he was certain of it, but her smile wasn't sly. She wasn't trying to trick him or win him over. No, her comment was more of an inward reflection and a hint of confusion. Wondering if Anton was really as good as he'd always claimed?

Hardly.

As quickly as Roman formed the impression, her expression changed and he was looking at a different woman, one who seemed open and engaging, her cares forgotten in favor of enjoying a lively conversation.

"I'm certainly not intuitive with them. Someone had to show me how to set up my email on my tablet."

And there was the "I'm harmless" claim Roman had been anticipating since he had realized who she was.

The conversation moved on to contacts and wedding arrangements. Iced coffees replaced the white wine everyone had sipped with lunch. Huxley said something about the dock and took Ingrid to inspect it.

Melodie made no move to follow, choosing instead to shift forward slightly and remove her sweater, revealing a matching sleeveless top that clung lovingly to her breasts as she twisted to drape the sweater over the back of her chair.

"I didn't expect it to be this warm. It's fall at home. Quite wet and chilly." She sat straight and, as if she felt the chill across the Atlantic, her nipples rose against the pale lemon of her top.

A base male fantasy of baring those breasts formed in his mind. He saw pink tips resembling cherries melting off scoops of ice cream. He wasn't a breast man per se, but the languid image of caressing and licking the swells, working his way to the sweet, shiny niblet at the peak, was so tangible he had to part his thighs to accommodate the pool of erotic heat that poured into his groin.

At the same time he realized conversation had stopped. She was very still.

He lazily brought his gaze up and realized she'd caught him blatantly ogling her. A strange jolt hit him like an electrical charge, deep in his gut and far stronger than a zing of static. It was like a full current that reverberated in his chest, making his heart skip a beat and his abdomen tighten.

Her blue eyes held his, fathomless and not the least offended. In fact, her reaction to his masculine interest was arousal. He'd seen it in the tightening of her nipples and read it now in the confused shimmer of excitement and indecision expanding her pupils. Her lashes quivered, eyes shiny, and the tip of her tongue wet her lips.

The pull behind his thighs became more insistent. He wondered if he had ever experienced a more carnal moment.

She swallowed and jerked her gaze from his as though it was a physical wrench of muscle from bone.

He mentally berated himself for letting her see his interest, highly irritated by how easily she had got to him. It was time to drop the ax.

"Does, um, he come around the office much?" she asked, gaze scanning restlessly toward the water. "Are you used to their displays?"

"Who?" he almost growled, then remembered two other people were here. Ingrid and Huxley. They held hands and bumped shoulders as they staggered, love drunk, across the sand.

Roman was behaving almost as inebriated, forgetting they were even here, manufacturing lurid fantasies of possessing a woman too lethal to imbibe. He tried to shrug away the strongest wave of sexual attraction he'd ever felt toward a woman and almost wondered if she'd slipped him something.

"He might, but I don't," he replied belatedly, forcing his mind back to the conversation. "The whole point in being on the cutting edge of technology is to use it." He chinned upward to his office, rebaiting his hook. "I often telecommute."

"And Ingrid is your avatar in New York?" she guessed.

That took him by surprise. He almost chuckled, then caught himself, dismayed by how easily she kept disarming him. He eyed her, searching for the source of her power. "I hadn't looked at it that way. I suppose she is."

"Working from home always seemed so ideal to me," she mused, propping her chin on her hand. "But now I'm doing it, I find I'm becoming a workaholic, never letting it go. I keep sitting down for one more thing and losing another two hours."

"You live alone, then," he said, picking up on what he thought she wanted him to deduce. It shouldn't please him to hear she was single. She was nothing to him, certainly not a woman he'd bed. Not in these circumstances. Perhaps his libido found her leggy build stimulating. That faint scent of citrus and roses emanating from her skin was pure seduction, but as much as he hated her family and wanted revenge, he wouldn't stoop to grudge sex. He didn't intend to touch her.

She could go ahead and offer herself, though. Rejecting her advances would make for a delightful twist. He wondered if she'd take this game of hers that far, and decided he would make it easy for her to humiliate herself.

A pulse of expectancy tugged at him.

This was a chess match, not a flirtation, he reminded himself.

"I do," she answered, fingertips grazing the pearls at her throat where he thought he saw her pulse fibrillating. Her glance went to the house. He suspected she was mentally recalling whether she'd seen evidence of a paramour in there. She hadn't. He kept his companions out of his private space.

"Me, too," he provided.

Melodie's flushed cheeks darkened with a deeper blush as she cut a glance toward him, perhaps trying to work out whether his remark was a signal of attraction.

There was no use pretending otherwise. She'd already caught him lusting, so he let her see that, yes, something in him found her appealing. He didn't understand how it could happen when he held her in such contempt, but he rather enjoyed the fact that she was so disconcerted by her own response as she read his interest. Her reaction was too visceral to be fake, which was probably why he was aroused by it.

It was a bad case of misguided chemistry. She certainly wasn't desirable to his rational mind, but maybe it was the risk of the situation that he found compelling. He'd developed a taste for plundering in his early years. Not of women. He was actually very cautious with how he approached relationships, but he loved finessing his way past defenses, exposing closely guarded secrets. He liked to prove he could. It filled him with enormous satisfaction.

"Where is home?" he asked. He'd read the answer yesterday, but he liked seeing how his attention put her in a state of conflicted sexual awareness.

"Virginia," she answered, smile not sticking. "For now. I'm considering a move to New York, though."

"Don't bother," he said instinctively, then closed his mouth in distaste at reacting so revealingly. "It's a perfectly livable city, but I don't care for it," he said in explanation. "More than my share of unpleasant memories," he added, to see if she'd pick up that the filthiest ones involved her family. Others were so heartbreaking he pushed them to the furthest reaches of his mind.

She only murmured, "I feel like that about Virginia."

Her tone exactly reflected his feelings, as though she'd opened the curtain and stepped inside the narrow space where he stored his soul. It was so disturbing he bristled, but she didn't seem to notice.

Her wrinkled brow relaxed and she forced a cheerful smile. "I need a fresh start. And you've inspired me now with your talk of telecommuting. Tell me how you manage it. Ingrid said you're a global company, so I assume you travel a lot? I expect I will, too, as I become more established. What are the pitfalls and best practices?"

She was very smooth in her way of bringing the conversation back to his business. He had to admire her for her dogged stealth.

"The happy couple is returning," he noted, avoiding answering by directing her attention to where Ingrid and Huxley had stopped at the far end of the pool, admiring the view of the beach.

Ingrid glanced at him, and he inferred that a consultation was requested.

He stood and held Melodie's chair, getting another eyeful of her breasts, not intentionally, but he was a man and they were right there.

Her sultry cloud of scent filled his nostrils, imprinting him with the image of marble and turquoise and sunlight off dishes so he would never forget this moment of standing here, her lithe frame straightening before him. She had a slender waist and hips he longed to grip so he could press forward, bend her to his will, cover and possess. He had to school himself against setting a proprietary hand on her back as they moved to where the bride and groom were debating logistics.

What the hell was it about her?

She moved with remarkable grace, he noted. Not so much skinny as long limbed. A thoroughbred. Not a mutt like he was. If he didn't have so much contempt for her bloodline, he might have questioned whether he was good enough for her.

Instead, he was the one with ethics while her sort wore an air of superiority that was only a surface veneer of respectability provided by old money. Perhaps she wasn't overt about thinking herself better than those around her, not the way her father had been, and perhaps she didn't act entitled, but she was among her own with Ingrid and Huxley. She took it for granted she was accepted. He couldn't help but appreciate that confidence.

"Would the guests moor here overnight?" Huxley asked.

"That's up to Mr. Killian," Melodie deferred, turning to him.

"Roman, please," he said drily. She could use his first name until he made his position clear, which would be about five minutes from now. "There's a shoal to be wary of," he said to Huxley, stepping forward so he could point.

He was fully aware of Melodie's proximity to his own. He had no intention of bumping her, though, and actually reached out absently to ensure he didn't.

Melodie was the one who recoiled in surprise, taking a hasty step backward.

He caught the movement out of the corner of his eye, heard her squeak of shock and snatched again, more deliberately.

She was already tipping backward. He missed her, tried again. Their fingertips brushed, but he failed to catch her. Her face pulled into a cringe as she fell backward into the deep end of the pool. Roman stepped back from the splash and stared at her one shoe caught in the grate.

CHAPTER THREE

ONCE MELODIE REALIZED her fall was inevitable, she let it happen, only splaying out her arms and holding her breath. Above her, through the rippled water, three blurry faces stared. Roman was throwing off his jacket and looking as if he might dive in.

She let herself sink, waiting until her foot tapped the bottom, then kicked herself back to the surface.

What an idiotic thing to do!

But that damned Roman had been throwing her for a complete loop, being all masculine and sexy, sending mixed messages of lust and disapproval, hovering next to her like a raptor, smelling tangy and male. She'd been standing next to him, admiring his build, thinking his voice was too hypnotic, when he'd reached toward her as if he knew she was there, as if he was a lover searching for the hand of his mate.

Her reaction had been startled fear that she'd betray how thoroughly he was affecting her if he touched her. She'd jerked back and...

"Pah!" she spat as she came up for air. "You might want to change the design of that grate before the wedding. Either that or we advise all the women to skip the stilettoes and wear flip-flops."

Ingrid and Huxley laughed unreservedly. Roman wore a more severe look.

It wasn't easy to tread water in a narrow skirt. Her second shoe came off as she kicked toward the edge.

Roman squatted as she reached for the lip of the pool. His strong hand grasped her forearm, dragging her closer whether she wanted his help or not. His other hand got hold of her opposite arm and he pulled her up and out of the pool as though she was a teensy ballerina, not a five-foot-ten mermaid pushing a hundred and thirty pounds. *Soaking wet*, she added with a private cringe.

Water sluiced off her, and she rather wished he had let her take stock before landing her in front of him, dripping and plastered with wet clothes, not a single thing left to the imagination. Her makeup had to be running and— Okay, good. Her pearls were still here, but seriously. She felt absurd.

She crossed her arms to hide the way her nipples hardened and risked a quick sweep of her gaze around the faces goggling at her. Ingrid was still snickering, hand cupped over her mouth while her eyes danced with laughter.

"What on earth, Mel?" she asked.

"You left your shoe on the bottom, Cinderella," Huxley teased, moving to where a large net lay against the low garden wall.

"I can't believe I did that," Melodie grumbled, mortified but able to laugh at herself. It was so ludicrous.

Roman didn't seem to think it was funny, though. He was staring at her so hard her wet clothes should have been nuked off her body.

"May I have a towel?" she prompted.

"Of course." He snapped into motion.

"Oh! I have a bathing suit you can wear," Ingrid exclaimed. "I bought it yesterday and left it in my bag." She disappeared into the house and Melodie shook her head. It was far too late for swimwear.

She followed Roman into the nearby cabana where he

turned with a towel in his hand. His gaze raked down her
again, making her acutely aware of how her clothes were
suctioned to her like a second skin. She plucked at her
knit top, which only stretched the neckline and ruined it.

Roman came forward, shaking out the towel and sling-
ing it around her. He was so tall it was no problem at all
for him to get it around her.

Her heart did another somersault and his musky scent
stole through the air of chlorine as his wide chest filled
her vision. Weakness attacked her.

"I—" It would be silly to apologize. She hadn't fallen
on purpose, but he looked so thunderous. "Thank you" was
all she could manage as he drew the edges of the towel to
where her waiting fingers brushed his.

"When you sank like that, I thought I was going to have
to come in after you."

"It was quite refreshing, to be honest. I needed to cool
off."

She shouldn't have said that. The sexual tension she was
fighting became something they both had to acknowledge,
like it was a real thing holding them in its vortex.

She found herself staring at his mouth, anticipating its
feel against hers. Kisses were about as far as she went these
days after losing her virginity for all the wrong reasons.
Even kisses, however, always seemed to fall short of the
hype. She always felt as though she was going through
the motions, not really losing herself to the experience. If
she couldn't get caught up in that much, there was no use
going further, she'd decided.

But she remained ever hopeful that she'd find a man
who made things different. Today, at least, she *wanted* to
be kissed. Deep longing filled her, making her ache to
know how it would feel to kiss the man before her.

Distantly she was aware of his hand grasping her upper
arm. He stepped closer. His head tilted.

She should have been startled, but it felt so natural. She dampened her lips. Parted them. And gasped when he branded her with the heat of his mouth.

So hot, so smooth and commanding, instantly hungry. Claiming her like a desert warrior stealing her for his pleasure. His hand splayed in a firm pressure behind her tailbone, bringing her imperiously into the wall of his muscled frame.

Heat burned through her wet clothing, sealing them tight with only the friction of dampened fabric between them.

He kissed her as though he meant it. As though he was making sure she'd never forget this moment. As though she was his and he was ensuring she knew it.

She kissed him back with the same passion, not thinking of anything beyond exploring this new pleasure. Letting him have her because what he was doing to her was fresh and exciting and incredible. His kiss made her feel desired. His tongue touched hers and shivers of delight stung her skin. A flood of arousal seared between her thighs, urged her to lean into him and let a moan of pleasure fill her throat.

"Here you are—oh!" Ingrid said on a breathless burst, then laughed with embarrassed hysteria.

Roman jerked back, keeping one hand on Melodie's arm to steady her. His firm grip hadn't hurt her, but his touch left a tingling impression. She massaged the spot, trying to dispel the odd vibration while she noted the front of his clothing wore her moist imprint.

"I'll come back," Ingrid offered, grin mischievous.

"No," Roman blurted, brushing past Ingrid as he moved swiftly out of the cabana.

Ingrid, nearly doubled over she was laughing so hard, she stepped and pulled the curtain across. *"O. M. G,"* she said with exaggerated significance, eyes huge.

Melodie dropped her burning face into her damp hands, eyes closed in mortification. "I don't know how that happened," she groaned.

"Oh, please," Ingrid chortled. "He's Roman Killian. You should see what the office looks like when it's announced he'll be in. It's like a red-carpet event, there are so many women wearing push-up bras and designer labels. I'm not the least bit surprised you—pun intended—*fell* for him."

"No, I haven't…" Melodie tried to protest, but her bones were still weak, and if Roman had walked back in and told her to come with him, she would have gone without a second thought.

"Don't bother," Ingrid instructed with a shake of her head. "If I hadn't been crushing on Huxley my entire life, *I* would have fallen for Roman. He's gorgeous. What intrigues me, though," Ingrid lowered her voice to murmur, sidling closer with a little wiggle of excitement across her shoulders, "is the way *he* is falling for *you*."

Melodie shook her head. "You're mistaken—"

"He can't take his eyes off you," Ingrid insisted, enjoyment gleaming in her eyes as she gave Melodie's drowned-rat state a good once-over. "To be fair, I don't see him with women very often. I think he's the sort who compartmentalizes. Work. Play. Know what I mean?" Ingrid made little stalls with her hands. "But when I have seen him with a date, he keeps up that aloof facade of his, never planting one on them as if he can't wait for everyone else to leave. And they're always blonde and stacked. Kittenish. Not really striking me as his intellectual equal."

"I fell into the pool, Ingrid. Hardly a sign of great intelligence," Melodie argued, heart galloping at the idea that Roman had been unable to resist kissing her.

She was *not* the type to provoke men to passion. Most of them thought she was too tall and wiry. Her half brother had done a number on her as a child, tearing her self-esteem to shreds in a way she'd only been able to rebuild once she had left home, so she still considered herself an ugly duckling who'd arrived at goose, not swan.

That dented self-esteem, along with her mother's need of her, had kept her from a serious pursuit of love, but she longed for a deep connection with the opposite sex. With her mother gone, there was more than just a hole in her daily schedule. She felt her single status very keenly. The sight of couples and families made her feel very lonely. She wanted someone to share her life with. Not the facade of a shared life that her parents had had, but the sort of deep, abiding love that Ingrid and Huxley had.

She opened the towel and wrapped it like a turban on her head, throwing off self-pitying thoughts as she peeled away her wet clothes.

Ingrid pulled the tags off the bathing suit and something else that she held up for inspection. "Look. Huxley bought a shirt. You can borrow this, too."

Any relief Melodie felt evaporated a moment later. Ingrid was decidedly smaller than she was. The bikini would be microscopic even on her client. On Melodie, it was downright lewd.

Ingrid was not deterred. She dropped Huxley's sleeveless white shirt over Melodie's head. "It's a bit risqué, but nothing I wouldn't wear poolside or to the beach."

Or in the bedroom to incite her fiancé?

Melodie looked at the thin fabric hanging from narrow straps over her shoulders to scoop low across her breasts and waft in an indecently high hem across her thighs, barely covering her bottom. Even on the beach, this outfit would be nothing less than bait. With the pearls resembling puka shells around her neck, she looked like a surfer groupie trolling for a vacation hookup.

Unfastening the necklace, she muttered, "I can't believe this has happened. I look so unprofessional."

"It's fine. Better than fine. Your legs should be licensed as a deadly weapon," Ingrid said with a meaningful lift of her brows. "Let's see if Roman likes them," she added with a wicked grin, gathering up Melodie's wet clothes and zipping outside with them, leaving the curtain to the cabana open.

Melodie hesitated, not wanting to be so encouraged by what Ingrid had said about Roman's interest. She really wasn't very experienced with men. Aside from her insecurities, a lot of the reason was exactly what she'd told Roman: she was a workaholic. She'd been supporting herself a long time, spending what little extra time she had visiting her mother, advocating for her. The few men she'd been loosely involved with had been nice enough, just not the type to inspire her to make room in her life for them.

Not that she expected Roman to want a place in her life! Quite the opposite. He struck her as a man who expected his women to be self-sufficient and sophisticated. Which she definitely wasn't—not when it came to relationships. She might not be an actual virgin, but she was a one-time wonder, still not sure what had possessed her to go through with it the first time.

Well, realistically, she knew that immaturity and helpless fury had driven her. She'd wanted to strike back at Anton and had wound up hurting herself and a man who hadn't deserved to be used. Anton's *friend*, a young man Anton had been using so he could party on his family's yacht, had had a crush on Melodie. She'd reveled in the opportunity to show Anton that not only did his friends find her attractive after all, but she had the power to influence them. She'd made the boy turn down Anton's demand to sail in favor of taking her for a private cruise. She went through with the lovemaking she'd promised him, but it had been awkward and disappointing. He'd realized she didn't truly care for him and had been quite devastated.

The entire experience had turned into a lesson in being kind to others and true to oneself, which she had tried to follow ever since.

Today, the truth was she might not know Roman enough to care deeply about him, but she was fiercely attracted to him. She wanted to sleep with him. Really wanted that more than she'd ever imagined possible.

With an impatient noise, she reached for the damp towel and slung it around her waist, needing the shred of added protection as she went out to face him.

He wasn't there, which made her heart sink in an alarming way.

"He went up to change," Huxley said, jerking his head toward the balcony, adding with a smirk, "Probably having a cold shower, too."

Ingrid finished hanging Melodie's wet clothing across the back of the chairs and said to Huxley, "If we're going to test those jet skis you reserved, we'd better run. You can get a cab, can't you, Mel? We're going the opposite direction to the hotel. We'll see you tomorrow at the meeting with the hotel manager about the room block."

Could she *be* more obvious? Melodie liked Ingrid, but at this moment she wanted to push *her* into the pool. *Don't leave me alone with him.*

But the customer was always right, she reminded herself.

Scanning her gaze across the table, she looked for her phone and realized all she had was her credit card in the pocket of her sweater—which was dry, at least. Thank goodness she had *that* much.

"Sure," Melodie said with a stiff smile, as if she was still wearing her conservative suit and had this situation fully under control.

"Bye!" Ingrid blew a kiss, grabbed her fiancé's sleeve and hauled him away.

Blushing with embarrassed annoyance, Melodie contemplated whether to head into the kitchen and ask the chef to call her a cab or stick around to see if Roman wanted to finish kissing the daylights out of her.

Okay, her hormones cried excitedly.

She had to get out of the sun. She was blistering.

Moving to the bottom of the outside stairs, she wavered, but told herself she couldn't leave without at least saying goodbye.

Yes, wanting to see him again is all about good manners, she mocked herself.

She climbed with trepidation, heart pounding as though she was descending the basement stairs in a thriller movie. So silly. He wasn't going to attack her. That kiss had been a surprise, but invited and totally mutual. She had wallowed in it.

The part of her that wanted it to happen again and maybe go further was what scared the daylights out of her. She wasn't that girl. She wasn't blasé about intimacy. She wasn't desperate or angry or deluding herself into love at first sight.

She was just really, really enticed by everything about him.

As she reached the top of the stairs, she grew cautious, feeling like a burglar, afraid she'd catch him indisposed.

"Roman?" she tried.

A very deliberate noise sounded, like someone striking a single key on a keyboard, hard. "Yes," he said from his office.

"I'm afraid I have to ask you to call me a cab." She tried to act casual as she moved forward. "I didn't bring my phone and…"

She came even with the open doors of the office and discovered him standing before his clear screens. He had changed, dispensing with a shirt altogether, and now wore only a pair of drawstring linen pants that hung with rakish sexiness off his hips, accentuating his smooth, powerful back and the curve of his buttocks.

"I'd ask Ingrid for hers, but she and Huxley just left…" She could hardly speak. Her throat had gone dry.

He turned. His flat abs and nicely developed chest fixated her. Animal attraction gripped her.

Why? She didn't understand it, and lifted her gaze to his, trying to work out where this attack of sexual craving was coming from.

He was scanning down her low neckline, taking in the outline of tiny triangles that barely covered her nipples beneath the translucent cotton, eyeballing the towel that she gripped around her hips.

His Adam's apple worked. "Why are you here, Melodie?" His tone was graveled with intolerance and something almost erotic. Desire?

"I— What do you mean?"

"Here, in my home." He joined her on the balcony, confrontational and ominous, arms and shoulders tanned and powerful, bare feet planted firmly. "Why are you here?"

"The wedding," she stated, nerves strummed by the suspicion in his tone.

"Be honest."

"What do you mean? I didn't *plan* this," she said, waving at her borrowed garb, suddenly realizing how it could look. But she hadn't made this happen. She wasn't using it as an excuse to stick around and throw herself at him. Not really. Okay, maybe she was throwing herself at him a little, but—

Oh, good grief. Could this get any worse?

"I didn't bump you," he bit out, eyes narrowing. "I didn't even touch you."

"No, I know. I was just…nervous," she stammered, attacked by the same hit of discomfiture that had made her avoid him by the pool. She'd instinctively known his touch would have a devastating effect on her. She'd leaped back from his reaching hand as though he could have burned her. He *had* burned her. When he'd kissed her in the cabana, the contact had seared all the way to her soul.

"Nervous," he charged, brows elevating as if he'd caught her out. "Why?"

Because he was a force, not a man. Her reaction to him was so strong it petrified her.

"You're different," she hazarded, but couldn't explain it even to herself.

"How?"

Boy, he was like an extension of his technology with those robotic commands for more information.

She crossed her arms, annoyed, but Ingrid's words were ringing in her ears. Was he reacting to her and feeling as out of sorts by this situation as she was?

The thought brought a soaring of buoyancy that she quickly tried to tame. A million things were running through her head, all her thoughts coming back to the fact that she was finally meeting a man who made her feel alive. She was interested and excited. Running away like a teenage girl too shy to speak to him would be silly. She'd kick herself forever if she did that. They were grown-ups. She was, by nature, an honest person.

"I find you attractive," she admitted, and immediately blushed. It was as if she'd deliberately stepped onto a gangplank high over the concrete. Her footing seemed wobbly and threatened to drop her into a hard fall.

"Do you," he disparaged.

His tone peeled a layer off her composure. She told herself she was being mature and didn't have enough invested to have anything to lose, but her self-respect grew thin and strained. *Bug eyes. Don't talk to my friends. They all think you're ugly anyway.*

At the same time, she put herself into Roman's shoes and thought she knew the source of his cynicism. "If you think I'm making some kind of awkward play for the rich guy, that's not true."

"You'd think I was just as attractive if I lived in a cardboard shack in a back alley?" he scoffed, arms folding and chin coming up with arrogant challenge.

Dear Lord, he was attractive. Like a Greek god with all that burnished skin over toned muscle, his aura one of superiority and might.

She almost blurted out how she'd walked away from the sort of wealth and education that would have made any job unnecessary for the rest of her life. If he only knew how much contempt she reserved for powerful men and how sorry she felt for the women who loved them...

But all that was behind her, and this moment was only about her and him. Who they were in this moment.

"I might," she allowed with a weak shrug. This was a physical thing. She suspected no matter where she had encountered him, she would still be unable to control her response to him.

"You don't even know me," Roman derided. "Why—?" He bit off the word, looking out to the water, gripped by an angry frustration that went beyond his response to her. He closed his hand on the rail, trying to retain his grip on the situation.

But his gaze tracked unerringly back to Melodie. The low neckline of her shirt accentuated her slender neck and delicate collarbone, offering a teasing glimpse of the upper swells of her breasts. Her damp hair fell in waves around her bare face. She had the sensual innocence of a maiden from a primitive jungle culture, pure temptation in her open regard, Eve-like in her patience for him to succumb to the desire drumming through him. The message was subliminal and as irresistible as a siren's.

Come to me.

All he could think was, *This is a damned sight more than attraction.* He was blind with lust, trying to hang on to a cool head while his body still felt the writhe of hers nudging against his erection. She'd inflamed him with their kiss, promising untold pleasure, appealing straight to the basest part of him and completely undermining his capacity for logical thought.

Thank God Ingrid had interrupted them. He was disgusted with himself for kissing her in the first place, let alone allowing her response to ignite his own. The moment he'd walked away from her, he'd begun grasping for rationalizations to explain how he'd reacted so uncontrollably. Maybe he had it wrong. Maybe she wasn't Gautier's daughter. Maybe her presence here wasn't by design.

But he'd reviewed everything and it was all too neat. Her mother hadn't been in society in years, yet her funeral had been a who's who of the Eastern Seaboard. Melodie had not only started her new wedding business the minute she had put her mother to rest, but had immediately curried favor with an old family friend who *happened* to be the mother of his PA. The timing was *auspicious* indeed. And her fall into the pool, orchestrated so beautifully, allowing her to linger in his home while her clothes dried, was equally suspicious.

Not only that, since yesterday he'd learned that Gautier Enterprises was bleeding red ink by the gallon. And he'd turned up additional photos showing Melodie under her father's wing, all of them beautifully stoic in the face of her mother's death. Most significantly, sly moves were happening behind the scenes. Roman's customers were being offered exorbitant discounts if they signed exclusively with Gautier. False promises were being made about the performance of the most recent Gautier product, and dishonest warnings were circulating about Roman's.

A fresh rush of hatred had encompassed him a moment ago as he'd looked at a photo of her with her father. Grim anger coiled through him that Melodie had anything to do with the man. He wanted her to be real, not a weapon her father was wielding. Not a willing foot soldier against him.

And he hated himself for being susceptible to her. He'd fallen for Anton's lies once and was edging dangerously close to being taken in by Melodie's. It was intolerable.

He'd learned all her weak points, though. Her father might have insulated himself very thoroughly, but she was wide-open. All his plans were in motion. With a tap of a key, he had ensured Ingrid would pick up his email insisting she fire Melodie, and with another ensured Melodie would have no home to go back to in Virginia. The rest of the false front she'd built would collapse like a row of dominoes over the next hours and days.

All while she continued to look at him with those Bambi eyes soft with invitation, a hint of irreverent humor in her smile.

"How well do you usually know the women you're attracted to when you first meet them?" Melodie asked, pulling him back to the present moment.

Touché. He snorted, privately admitting that physical attraction was typically the reason he set out to learn a woman's name. Ironically, he had learned more about Melodie before he'd kissed her than he'd ever learned about most women he'd slept with.

Of course, he'd been more attracted to Melodie at first glance than he'd ever been before. He'd only become more intrigued as each minute had passed. And now, despite everything he knew, despite already taking steps to crush her plans, he could barely take his eyes off her breasts, rising and falling in a shaken tremble that was utterly fascinating.

The basest male in him wanted to kiss her again. Feel her under him. Be inside her and see how high the flames would fan.

"Do you think I'm not struggling with this, too? I don't kiss strangers. I don't..." She offered a helpless palm, averting her face so he only saw a look of confusion and longing in the profile she turned to the water.

The rest of her was pure temptation, nipples peaking in excitement beneath the tiny red bikini top. Her legs went on forever and his hand itched to find the skin beneath the drape of that oversize, yet completely inadequate, shirt. He was hardening at the thought.

"I just keep wondering how else you get to know someone except by spending time with them?" Her gaze came back to his, earnest and unsure.

He shook his head, amazed by how good an actress she was, relieved on some level that she wasn't genuine because he would have to do some serious soul-searching before involving himself with such a multifaceted yet sincere woman. He wasn't cut out for relationships with a future. That was why he was careful how and when he fell into the loose ones he did enjoy.

Fortunately she was a huckster peddling a shell of such relationships, amazing him with her tenacity and smooth attempts to manipulate him, her mouth trembling in a struggle to smile as she offered a hesitant, "Of course, if it's not a mutual thing, I'll..."

She took a few steps closer, gaze drifting to the patio below, lashes lowering and brow pulling together in a wince of rejection.

He didn't move. How could she be this good? How could he be feeling like this? He didn't want anything to do with her, but he wanted to understand why he was this easily taken in so he could guard against such things further down the road.

"What do you really want from me, Melodie?" he asked in his deadliest tone, willing her to come clean.

"Just, um… Honestly?" She blinked up at him, practically virginal with her defenseless gaze, her mouth working to find words. "For you to kiss me again," she said, her voice a thin husk. "To see if…" She licked her lips, leaving an expectant silence.

"Come and get it, then," he said gruffly, trying to scoff, telling himself he was only seeing the extent she'd go to in this industrial espionage of hers, letting her demean herself when he had every intention of rejecting her.

But it didn't happen that way.

She absorbed his command with a small flinch, then lifted her chin as though gathering her courage. As she stepped up to him, her hands opened on his rib cage in a feathery tickle that made his entire body jerk in reaction. His nipples hurt, they pulled so tight. She was tall enough that when she lifted on tiptoes, her mouth easily met his.

She pressed pillowy lips to his. He told himself to shove her back and tell her—

The rocking of her mouth parted his lips. He caught the first damp taste of her and his tongue shot out instinctively, greedily plunging into her mouth the way he wanted to plunge into her body. He closed his arms around her, pulled her into him with a strength he barely remembered to temper, and slanted his mouth to take full possession of hers.

She opened to him, arched and pressed into him and moaned capitulation.

Rational thought evaporated in a groan of craving.

CHAPTER FOUR

MELODIE HAD JUST wanted to see, that was all. See if he really did make her feel like this. See if something special existed between them.

But, oh, things raced out of control quickly. As their lips met and the kiss took hold, she stopped thinking, only vaguely aware that no man had ever run his hands over her skin like this. Such strong hands. Such an amazing feeling to be petted and shaped, firm fingers digging in as he pinned her tightly to his naked chest, then explored her with a touch like velvet.

Her body's reaction was a study in biology, skin growing so sensitive his touch was almost abrasive, yet inciting at the same time. She could feel the scrape of his chest hair through the light shirt she wore, could feel the burn of his body heat, and even though she could barely stand the conflagration, she wanted to be closer and closer still. Her arms went around his neck so she was belly to belly with him, loins to—

He was hard.

His hands cupped her buttocks and his teeth closed on her nape, making her bones turn to sand while she rubbed instinctively against that hard ridge. Something deeper than desire, a craven need, punched like a blow right there, where she felt him against her most private flesh. The ache was hurtful and demanding. Nothing like she had ever felt. Never had sensations overwhelmed her like this. It was stunning, absorbing, erasing all thoughts except primal want. *Please. More. Now.*

Her fingers went into his hair. She was pure reflex, wanting his mouth over hers, wanting to open and give and take.

He smothered her with his passionate, hungry kiss, hands smoothing up the contracting muscles in her belly to cup her breasts, making her sob with relief at the pressure of his touch on those tender, aching orbs. The cups of the bathing suit went askew and then he had her bare breasts in his palms, massaging, fondling, rubbing at her nipples so streaks of white-hot arousal shot straight into her loins.

She whimpered, seeking pressure where desire was pooling like thick lava. She didn't know how to tell him, only knew that his skin was as taut as a drum under her searching hands, his tongue erotic as he played with hers. A distant part of her wondered how this was happening, but another part didn't care, only wanted him to keep touching her, keep playing with her nipples, keep stirring and stimulating her.

His hand went to her hip and eased the bathing suit down. He stepped back to look as the bottoms dropped around her ankles. Watching his own hand, he slid his touch to the front of her thigh, up to her belly, then down, fingers combing, pressing—

"Oh!" she gasped, never having felt her body respond like this. Sharp and wicked and wanton sensations prickled through her as he sought with a fingertip and toyed with her, pulling her in for another kiss with a hand behind her neck, utterly devastating her with the waves of pleasure he was rocketing through her.

She caressed him with restless hands, wanting to touch everywhere at once, wanting to fill her palms with him, wanting to excite him the way he was doing to her. She no sooner cupped his hard shaft through linen, though, and his hand bumped hers, ceasing to caress her so he could release his drawstring.

His pants fell and he stepped out of them, completely naked. He was ferociously aroused, dark and thick and ready. She hadn't got a proper glimpse of her first lover, and Roman wiped all thoughts of the past from her mind. He fascinated her.

She wasn't frightened. No hint of hesitation struck. She was pure eagerness and excitement as she took in his nude frame, so perfect he was like a statue sculpted by a master, formidable and flawless, rampant and ferociously masculine.

Catching her up hard against his front, he lifted her as he moved, muscles shifting under her hands as he held her nose to nose, feet off the ground and dangling. His mouth nipped at hers, inciting her to kiss him back. She curled her arms around his neck, ran her tongue over his bottom lip, then drew on it, sucking flagrantly, liking the way his hands hardened on her. He took the few steps to his bed where he followed her to the mattress, spreading her legs as he came down over her.

Yes, she thought. It was the only word in her head. Her body was in a state of undeniable demand. Her entire being yearned for the feel of Roman's hard muscles and his weight and *yes*. The feel of his aroused flesh rubbed against hers, parting and arousing, teasing and dampening. Seeking.

Her arms cradled his head, her mouth pulled at his parted lips, licking and panting as he breathed raggedly along with her, breaths mingling, their gasps and growls carnal and unfettered.

With a blind, startled shake of his head, he drew back. "I didn't—"

"Don't stop," she cried, arching to offer herself where

she could feel him ready to penetrate, needing him inside her. She was so aroused she would die, actually die, if he didn't keep pressing *right there.* "Please, Roman, please."

He groaned and the insistent pressure increased. Her tight flesh gave way, parting and accepting.

Oh. It had been a long time and this was… Burning. Intimate. So much more like she'd always wanted it to be. His length pushed in, filling her, making her hold still to savor, wanting all of him…

With a growl, he opened his mouth against her neck, drawing a love bite up to the surface of her skin. She practically levitated off the bed, pressing up into him, surrendering utterly to the experience. His tongue licked against the artery pounding in her throat and he shuddered as his body came flush against hers, pressing tight, possessing her to the limits of their joined flesh.

She closed her trembling legs around his hips, astonished, beyond aroused. Mindless. She was pure sensation, her only dim thought that she was happy it was like this. Pure, abject passion infused the moment.

He lifted his head and looked at her, eyes fogged with passion. Something clouded his gaze, as if he was becoming aware of how fast they'd arrived at this point.

She didn't care about that. It was supposed to be like this. Animalistic, but with both of them caught up in overwhelming desire. She licked her lips.

His gaze followed the signal and his head bent.

They were lost again. Kissing deeply. Her body eased its tight grasp on his, inviting him to move. He did, muscles trembling, and his excitement fueled hers. She stroked his back and rubbed her thighs against his sides and lifted her hips to accept the return of his, seeking pressure where she ached for it most.

He made a feral noise and moved with more deliberation, making her gasp at the sensation of friction and something that strummed the very heart of her. It was the most instantly addictive feeling she'd ever encountered. She made a noise of female ardor and encouraged him with primal arches and a grind of her hips. The more he moved, the more reality fell away. All she cared about was the next thrust and the next.

More. Now. Please. *Please*.

They writhed in ecstatic struggle, fighting to hold on to the moment, lascivious sounds filling the air as the intensity grew, as he moved faster, as climax approached with merciless demand.

The paroxysm struck her suddenly, holding her in a hard grip, mouth open in a silent scream. Sensations detonated then reverberated through her, rocking her to her core.

Roman's arms locked straight, a ragged cry of triumph tearing through the air as his hips sealed to hers and pulses of heat met her clasping orgasm, strengthening and prolonging her pleasure.

They were wholly attuned, joined in body and involvement. It wasn't happening to him or her. *They* were the experience.

With broken cries, they collapsed into weakness, sweaty and wrung out, panting and shaking. Tears of deep emotion leaked to dampen Melodie's lashes as she kept her eyes clenched shut, so shaken by the wildness of her actions she could barely face what they'd just done.

That had been...

She didn't have words.

That was—

Roman lifted off Melodie and pushed clumsily to his feet, arms weak, knees shaking. The friction of leaving her was a pleasurable stroke that turned to the chill of loss. He had to turn away to keep from falling under her spell all over again.

No condom. He turned away, aghast at his carelessness. He never forgot, never lost his head. He liked sex, but he was always, *always* aware of protection.

He'd started to pull away as he felt her naked flesh against his pulsing erection. She was the one who'd yanked him back into the act, begging. Offering herself with such abandon he'd discarded all cares but getting inside her.

He shot a wary look her way, genuinely shaken by the way she'd slithered past his shields.

She'd rolled onto her side, but was still diagonal on the bed, knees together now, shirt pulled low to hide her nudity, head pillowed on her curled arm. Her big eyes blinked in sensual shock as she offered him a tentative smile.

"I've always wanted to be swept away by passion." Her languid tone was a caress and an invitation, as alluring as a drug to an addict. She made him want to join her, to lock out the world and let her become everything he needed.

Which was probably what she had planned. First, dull his senses with the kind of sex that reset the bar. Then lower his guard so he'd let her wander his home so she could, what? Dig through his files while he slept?

He had *not* meant to touch her. He hated himself for being weak enough to do so. He'd been on the verge of coming downstairs to spell out exactly how he was taking his revenge, but she'd come to him and coldcocked him with seduction.

A mix of emotions rose in him: contempt for both of them, fury, disappointment, a kind of defeat that took him back to a time when he'd been completely powerless... He *hated* feeling these things, especially all at once. With ruthless discipline, he shut himself down, refusing to be drawn by her sultry afterglow. Women were as vulnerable after sex as they were during, but he closed himself off to that, too.

Melodie must have read something in his look. Her lashes quivered and one hand tugged her shirttail down a little more. "Maybe it's always like that for you," she murmured self-consciously.

"It is," he lied flatly, unable to stomach how he'd let lust, for *her*, sweep him completely beyond himself. "I know who you are," he continued, before her flinch of defenselessness could have an impact on him. He strode across to gather his pants and stamped his feet into them, straightening to tie them into place with jerky movements. "You're wasting your time."

"What...? What do you mean?" She tucked her legs to the side as she sat up, brow furrowing.

"Charmaine Parnell-Gautier," he pronounced without inflection, as though they were exchanging information over a boardroom table. "I know your father and brother sent you here. Whatever you thought you could do to me isn't working. I'm three steps ahead of all of you." He picked up her discarded bikini bottom and brought it to the bed, placing it near her knee. "It's time for you to leave."

Her plump lips parted and her skin went so pale he thought she might faint. His heart lurched with alarm.

But she gathered herself quickly, drew a shaken breath and straightened her spine, shoulders going back.

"You think my father sent me here?"

"I know he did."

"You're wrong." Tilting her head at him in an admonishing stare, she looked him right in the eye. "My birth certificate says Garner Gautier is my father, but I don't have anything to do with him." Bitterness flashed in her expression. "I'm not surprised you might have a bone to pick with him. He buys friends and makes enemies, but whatever he's done to you has nothing to do with me."

Wow, he thought distantly. She certainly knew how to shuffle her hand and play a new card. He was supposed to be reassured, he imagined, by her pretending they had a common adversary.

"What he did was steal my work and lose me my home. I might believe you had nothing to do with his crimes if I hadn't spent yesterday afternoon reviewing recent photos of you two together."

Her lip curled in revulsion. She shook her head. "That's not what—"

"Melodie," he interrupted coldly. "This isn't a conversation. I don't *care* what you have to say. I'm simply telling you that your idea to use my PA to infiltrate my home has failed."

"I'm not *infiltrating*! I'm planning her wedding—"

"No. You're not," he informed, oddly empty of feeling as he served up the next slice of his revenge. This should feel good, but it just made him bitter. "I've instructed Ingrid to fire you. If she wants to hold her wedding here, which she does, she will find another planner. One who actually does this sort of thing for a living."

Melodie couldn't believe what she was hearing. Clammy fear was pulsing through her, killing her afterglow and beginning to make her feel dirty and cheap. She was sitting here half-naked, a very personal tenderness reminding her of what they'd been doing a few short minutes ago.

Snatching up the bathing-suit bottom, she tucked her feet into it and worked it up her legs, giving Roman her back as she pulled it into place. Her skin felt flayed under his regard, her inner self yanked into the open, kicked and spat on.

It was such a shock her mind could hardly make sense of it. All she knew was that this had something to do with her father and Anton. She knew all too well what a bitter taste they left in one's mouth. She clung to reason with her fingernails, tried to regain her poise and some semblance of control over this crazed situation.

She didn't sleep with strangers. She didn't—

Think, Melodie.

"You can't fire me," she said firmly. "I have a contract." She reached through the neckline of the shirt to straighten the bikini top. Where was her power suit when she needed it?

"Do *not* charge any cancellation fees," he warned. "If you try to recover any costs from this trip, if you so much as contact Ingrid to plead your case, I will make this worse than a job loss and eviction. Now go home, tell your father you failed and never come after me again."

"Stop," she insisted, spinning to confront him with an upraised hand, barely able to process what he was saying— *eviction*? She knew the cold fury and bloodlust that came of dealing with her father and half brother. Better than he ever would. She just needed to make him realize they were on the same side. "Roman, listen. I have *nothing* to do with him or Anton. Firing me will not impact them at all."

"It's time to leave," he said with quiet frost.

"They're not even going to know," she asserted, hearing the crack of growing emotion in her voice and clawing hard to keep her cool. It was really hard when voices in the back of her head were saying, *They're still doing it. They're still able to hurt you.* "What you're doing impacts me, not them."

"You're all one and the same." The Gautier lack of mercy left a virulent flatness behind his eyes. Broader understanding began to hit. He really thought she was some kind of spy. That she had been put up to this by her father and brother.

Oh, she vaguely knew what her brother did for a living. She'd never understood *how*. He was the furthest thing from a techno-genius, and now pieces were falling together. Of course Anton would have stolen the product that had filled his bank account. Of course her father would have covered for him and profited along with him.

"I don't know how to convince you, but you're wrong. Before you go through with all this, stop. Think about what you're doing. Give me a chance to explain."

"There's no stopping. It's done," he said matter-of-factly.

She swallowed, barely breathing, not wanting to believe him.

"You've already told Ingrid—"

"I emailed her before you reached the top of the stairs."

She shook her head, absorbing the magnitude of losing this contract. This wedding was supposed to put her on the map. She was finally starting a real job. A career she could feel excitement about. No more juggling two or three minimum-wage jobs at makeup counters or bistros. Her aspirations of finally moving into a decent apartment, maybe traveling because she wasn't tied down by her mother and debt, dimmed and doused like a candlewick gutting out, leaving only a wisp of smoke to sting her nostrils.

"You can't do this," she insisted numbly. Her mind leaped to wondering if she could start over somewhere, but as he'd pointed out, there was an investment in starting up a business like this. Without Ingrid's payment, she was in a very deep hole. Then there was the loss of Ingrid's circle of contacts. Starting over meant starting at the bottom, not stepping into a tony crowd with money and taste. "You're destroying my life," she informed him, heart beginning to tremble in her chest.

"Be sure to tell your father exactly how it feels."

He wasn't going to hear her on the lack of communication between her and Garner. She wouldn't bother mentioning it again. This *was* happening. She could see his resolve and, if dealing with her father had taught her nothing else, she had learned to accept that there was evil in this world. The best you could do was mitigate the damage.

Exactly what *was* the damage?

"What…?" She was afraid to ask. "What did you say about eviction?"

He folded his arms, feet planted firmly. "I've made an offer to the owner of your building, one he can't refuse. It's on condition that your unit be made available immediately."

Fury closed her fists into painful knots. "You can't *do* that."

He didn't react beyond saying, "Your things are being removed as we speak."

"To where?" she cried.

"The nearest Dumpster?" he offered with a pitiless shrug.

"You—" Her voice caught and realization began to squeeze her in its icy fingers. Fine quakes accosted her. She shook her head in convulsive denial as the buildup of emotion threatened to break the walls of her control. One thought formed and clung like a teardrop to a lash. "You're having my mother thrown in the Dumpster. Is that what you're saying? What the hell kind of man *are* you? There are *laws*."

His brows jerked together, the first sign of emotion since they'd been writhing with passion. "What do you mean?"

"My mother's ashes are in my apartment. You can't just throw someone away like that. You can't even—" Oh, what the hell did a man like him care about how hard it was to make the arrangements for scattering ashes?

Anxiety brought tears to her eyes, and she dashed them away, furious that she was breaking down, but this was the last straw. Losing things, starting over, having nowhere to live… Those were all problems she'd overcome before. Defiling her mother's remains was more than she could withstand. Her breath hissed in her pinched nostrils while her mind raced through all the hours of travel it would take to get back to Virginia to save her.

"I'll make a call," he said.

Because the wheels were already in motion.

It hit her that he'd been making these arrangements yesterday, long before he'd kissed her in the cabana. He had set up all these horrible things, consigned her mother to the Dumpster, then had sex with her. She recoiled as she realized he'd already been filled with hatred and thoughts of revenge as he'd carried her to this bed.

Her revulsion must have shown. He reacted with a dark flinch.

"I will," he assured her, glancing around as though he was looking for the nearest phone.

"You'll make a call," she repeated as she edged toward hysteria. "You're just full of consideration, aren't you, *lover*," she spat. The word tasted like bile.

"Do you want me to do it or not?" His gaze flashed back to hers with warning.

She was ready to take him apart with her bare hands and he must have known it. He tensed with readiness, stance shifting as he balanced his weight on his planted feet, darkly watchful. His lethal air should have terrified her, but she was pulsing with the sort of protective instincts that drove people to lash out in a blind rage. Her mother's well-being throbbed in her brain, urging her to injure and incapacitate in order to save. She wanted to hurt him. Badly. So badly.

Don't, a voice whispered in her head. *Don't be like them*.

"As if I'd trust you," she managed, voice wavering, whole body beginning to rack with furious shakes. "*I* will make a call," she said raggedly, knocking her breastbone with her knuckles. "I'll keep her safe. I'm the only one who ever has. The only reason I went back there was for her," she cried, throwing the truth at him like a grenade. "I swore I'd never set foot in that house again, but my father wasn't going to let me have her ashes unless I put on a state funeral and gave him those damned photos you're so convinced prove I'm here on his behalf. You think you're the only person they've ever hurt, Roman? Don't be so arrogant. You're not that special!"

She spun toward the door.

"Melodie," he ground out. "I'll call to make sure—"

"My friends call me Melodie. You can call me Charmaine. Like they do. Because you're just like them."

She went through the interior of the house. It was faster and allowed her to avoid going anywhere near him as she made her exit. She ran down the hall, blind to anything but a blur of yellowed marble and red carpet, barely keeping her footing on the stairs before she shot out the front door.

She heard her name again, but didn't look back. The paving stones were hot on her bare feet, burning her soles, but she barely felt the scorch and cut of the pebbles. Her only thought was that she needed to get away from him. Needed to get to her mother.

CHAPTER FIVE

THREE WEEKS LATER, Roman was in New York, conscience still smarting from everything that had happened with Melodie. Her final words—*you're just like them*—kept ringing in his head, growing louder as time progressed, cutting like a rope that grew tighter the more he struggled against it.

Initially, he'd thought she was merely twisting things around as she'd seen her plans falling apart. He'd had very little pity for her in those first postcoital moments, too angry with himself to hear that he might have computed things wrong.

The bit about her mother's ashes had bothered him, though. He had nothing of his own mother except vague, poignant memories of a woman who had seemed broken and defeated, voice filled with regret as she promised to get him back. Given how hard she'd tried to turn her life around, he'd felt doubly cheated when she had died before she was able to regain custody. The fact he'd only been informed of her death as an afterthought had been insult to injury.

He quickly turned away from those painful memories, frustrated that he couldn't seem to keep his mind plugged into work. It had always been his escape from brooding and he needed it more than ever.

Yet he found himself rising and stepping away from his desk to look over his view of Central Park. At least his eviction plans hadn't actually put the ashes in danger. As Melodie had pointed out, there *were* laws. His ability to have her things removed required thirty days' notice. She'd arrived home and cleared out within days, according to the building manager. Her mother's ashes had been safe the entire time, and Melodie had taken them with her when she'd left.

Twelve years ago, he *had* been thrown out of his home overnight, losing everything. The locks had been changed while he had hitchhiked from Virginia to New York, still nursing broken ribs and two black eyes after confronting Anton at his father's campaign office. His meager possessions had been gone when the super had let him into his apartment, not that he'd cared about anything except his custom-built computer. Taking that had been pure malice. They'd already had the files. They'd wanted to set him back, quite literally disarm him, and it had worked.

Roman hadn't dared go to the police. Not after Garner's threats of charging him with hacking. Roman had that prior conviction and no money to hire a lawyer. No time to wait for the wheels of justice to turn. Survival had been his goal.

Living on the streets, really understanding what his mother had been up against, he'd not only come to understand and forgive her, but he'd even considered a form of prostitution himself. The temptation had been high to sell his skills to the highest bidder and embrace a life of crime. Honest work hadn't been paying off.

Somehow, though, he'd found himself outside Charles's house—the security specialist who had helped him all those years ago. He'd walked as though he was being pulled toward a beacon, arriving without understanding why or how his feet had carried him that direction. Charles hadn't been there. He'd been in a home, suffering dementia. But his wife, Brenda, had let him in.

Until then, as a product of the foster system, Roman hadn't really believed things such as friendship and kindness and loyalty were real. He'd seen Charles's singling him out as a mercenary move, a specialist developing a skilled apprentice for his own benefit. Anton had befriended him to exploit him, as well. That was how it was done, Roman had thought. Nothing personal. People used people. That was how life worked.

But as Charles's wife had taken him in for no other reason than because Charles had always spoken fondly of him, Roman had begun to comprehend what one person could mean to another. Not that he took advantage of her. No, he had carried his weight, taking out the garbage and giving her what he could for groceries and rent every week.

She hadn't needed his money, though. She wasn't rich, but she was comfortable. She had grown children she saw often, so she wasn't lonely. The house had been well alarmed in a good neighborhood. She hadn't needed his protection. She'd had no legal obligation to help him.

She'd done it because she had a generous heart.

It had baffled him.

He still wondered what he might have resorted to if she hadn't taken him in for bacon and eggs. Told him to shower and provided him with clean clothes. If she hadn't listened to his story and believed him.

He'd been wary, not allowing her to be as motherly as she had wanted to be. Almost his entire life to that point had been a reliance on strangers. He hadn't wanted to go back to that kind of setup, but her unconditional caring had been a glimpse of what he had missed in losing his own mom. Parents, good ones, were a precious commodity.

So the thought of Melodie's mother's ashes being mistreated still bothered him, even though nothing terrible had come to pass. It had been more than the basic indecency of such a thing. He simply wasn't that cruel.

Meanwhile, the claim Melodie had made about how she'd come to have those ashes had shaken his assumptions about her and her family. He had needed to know more, to understand if what she had claimed about her estrangement from her father could be true. He'd made a number of calls over the ensuing days, first talking to her building manager at length.

Melodie, it seemed, was a perfect tenant who paid on time, lived quietly and took care of minor repairs herself. In fact, until the recent passing of her mother, she'd spent most of her days out of her apartment, working or visiting her mother at the clinic.

When Roman had looked more closely at her finances, he'd learned that she'd been living simply for years. Her income was low, especially for the daughter of a senator who received dividends from a global software company. For six years she had worked in a variety of part-time and minimum-wage jobs, only taking on debt to improve her mother's care and then to start her wedding planning business.

He'd spoken to Ingrid's mother, too, learning more about Melodie's mother than Melodie herself, but even that had been an eye-opener. Patience Parnell had been a fragile sort at college. She'd been given to tears and depression over the tiniest slight. She'd quit school when a modeling agency had scouted her, but after the initial boost to her self-esteem, that sort of work had ground her down. She'd left that career to marry a rich widower, expecting to be a homemaker and help him raise his son. Instead, she'd been his trophy wife, constantly on display as he set his aspirations on Washington. The demands of networking, campaigning and entertaining had grown too much for her. She never really recovered from postpartum depression after having Melodie. She'd checked into a sanitarium six years ago and, it was whispered, had checked out under her own terms.

When she had been diagnosed with breast cancer, she had refused treatment, letting it take her life in a type of natural suicide.

Every time he thought about it, he saw Melodie before him in that ridiculous outfit. Her anguish had been so real as she'd said, *I'll keep her safe. I'm the only one who ever has.*

That crack in her control was the thing that niggled most. She had been such a coolheaded fighter up to that point. He'd seen it in the way she'd doggedly tried to argue with him. At any other time he would have admired such a quick, clear ability to reason her way out of conflict. Hell, he probably would have tried to hire her. People who could step past emotion to straighten out a tense situation were gold.

All he'd seen at the time, however, was an attack. A cold-blooded one. His mind had been so skewed by his experience with her father and brother he'd stayed on the offensive, refusing to hear her, especially because she'd been so levelheaded in her defense. He'd read her wrong because, until those last moments, she hadn't flinched or broken down.

That strength in her had thrown him, making him see her as an adversary. Now all he could think about was how it would feel to put all one's energy into fighting for someone, for your *mother*, and lose her to a lack of will to live.

He swallowed, pushing stiff fists into his pockets, knuckles coming up against the string of pearls he should have returned to Melodie by now. He kept thinking she might contact him, but, in her shoes, would *he* want to talk to him?

If there was a good enough reason, he thought she would.

The beads rubbed mercilessly against his knuckles, the way a certain question kept rolling around in his mind, rubbing and aggravating.

Did no condom mean no birth control?

A lead blanket descended on him each time he recalled his fleeting moment of sobriety, as he had recognized the mistake he was about to make.

He was a man of logic. He didn't believe in giving in to feelings. He still couldn't understand how he had, especially with his view of Melodie as dark as it had been. He'd been appalled in those first seconds afterward for so much as touching her.

Yet it had been the most profound sexual experience of his life.

Had it been the same for her? Had their physical attraction been real? *Please, Roman, please.* His entire body clenched with tension and his breath drew in and held, savoring the memory of skin and musky scents and hot, wet welcome pouring over him like a bath. Behind his closed eyes, another question, the most burning question, glowed brightly.

Was she pregnant?

Beggars can't be choosers. It was a truth Melodie had learned to live with the day she'd come home six years ago to discover her father had badgered her mother into a hospital she couldn't leave.

She's an embarrassment, he'd said.

He was the embarrassment, Melodie had informed him. Terrible words had followed, ending with her nursing a bruised cheek, a sore scalp and a wrenched shoulder while she'd begged through choked-back tears for permission to see her mother. He'd forced her to stay silent on his abusive behavior if she wanted so much as a phone call.

After striking that deal, Melodie had walked out, going to a friend's house and never returning. Her privileged life had ended. She'd learned the hard way how to make ends meet, taking whatever job she could find to survive.

Of course, there was one job she had refused to stoop to, but today might be the day she completely swallowed her pride. They'd noticed at her temp office job that she had a flare for organization. They wanted to offer her a permanent position with a politician's campaign team. Become a handler. A political gofer. *Barf.*

But the money was significantly better than entry-level clerk wages.

And her mother's wish to have her ashes sprinkled in the Seine was weighing on her.

So Melodie begrudgingly put on a proper tweed skirt and jacket over a black turtleneck, put her hair in a French roll and closed the door on her new apartment far earlier than necessary so even if she missed her first bus, she wouldn't be late for her interview.

This was an old building, bordering on disrepair, and it smelled musty, but the price was right and all the locks worked.

As she walked down the stairs, she told herself to be thankful she had anything at all. After a lifetime of watching her mother struggle against negative thoughts and spirals of depression, Melodie had learned not to dwell on regrets or could-have-beens. She accepted her less-than-ideal circumstances philosophically and set goals for a better situation, confident she would get to where she wanted to be eventually. This apartment and taking a job she didn't want was merely a step in the process.

This was also the *last* time she started from scratch, she

assured herself, grateful her mother hadn't lived to see her fall on her face this way.

Mom. Pearls. France.

Her hand went to her collar, didn't find the necklace, and her heart sank into the pit of her stomach.

She tried not to think of France, but Roman crept into her thoughts day and night, taunting her with how horribly she'd misjudged him.

She blamed her sunny ideals. All her life she had wanted to believe deep emotional connections were possible, even though her mother's yearning for a better love from her father had been futile. And even though, among the loose friendships Melodie had made over the years, she'd seen more heartbreaks than success stories.

Ingrid and Huxley had fed her vision, though. Every once in a while, she came across a couple she wished she could emulate: the people who communicated with a glance and did sweet things for each other, just because.

The only way she'd coped with her barren early years had been by promising herself that real, true love would come to her eventually.

She'd mistaken a sexual reaction for a signal of mental and emotional compatibility where Roman was concerned. Maybe she wasn't as delicate as her mother had always been, but grief had been taking its toll. A month past her out-of-character encounter with Roman and she could see how susceptible she'd been that day. Ingrid's joy in her coming nuptials had created impatience for a life partner in Melodie. She'd seen the possibility of a future in a kiss from a superficially attractive man.

Relationships, she decided, could wait until both her finances *and* her heart were back on their feet. The thought allowed her to feel resilient as she reached the ground floor. She was capable of meeting challenges head-on with equanimity. She would take this job and rebuild her life.

After striding across the lobby, she pushed open the glass door onto the street.

The bluster of a nor'easter yanked it out of her hands.

Actually, it was a man. He filled the space, blocked her exit. He wore a suit and an overcoat. His dark hair glistened with rain. He was clean shaven and green eyed like a dragon. Heart-stoppingly gorgeous.

Roman Killian.

Melodie was still in Virginia, but had moved to Richmond.

The moment that detail had been reported to Roman, he'd booked a flight. The dry, musty interior of her apartment building, with its ugly red-and-silver wallpaper, closed around him as he stepped into the foyer, forcing her back several steps into the wall of mailboxes. He barely took in his surroundings. He was too busy studying her.

She looked…thin. A stab of worry hit him as he considered what that could mean for an unborn baby. Her face was wan, too, beneath her makeup. She wore a smart suit beneath an open coat, but her eyes swallowed her face. Her pale lips parted with shock. Whatever she held dropped from her grip with a muffled thump.

It was just her purse, but he shot forward in instinctive chivalry.

She snatched it before he could, jerking upright to stare down on him.

It was the oddest moment of juxtaposition. *She* was the one living in a low-end ZIP code in a modest suburb of the city. *He* appeared on list of Fortune 500 CEOs as one of the richest men in the world. His suit was tailored, his handkerchief silk.

Yet Melodie stood above him like a well-born lady. Which she was.

He knelt like a peasant. A scab on the complexion of society.

Which he was.

He held her gaze as he rose, shedding any traces of inferiority. Refusing to wear such a label. Not anymore. The struggle to get here had been too long and too hard.

Her eyes grew more blue and deep and shadowed as he straightened to his full height. He found himself resisting the urge to smile as they stood face-to-face. He'd forgotten she was so tall. She met his eyes with only the barest lift of her chin. And she impacted upon him with nothing more than turmoil and silence.

The same fascination accosted him that he'd suffered in France. He was instantly ensnared. If anything, her pull was stronger. Now he knew what it felt like to kiss her and touch her, to possess her and release all of himself into her. The power she had over him was deeply unsettling. Through air coated in layers of old carpet and must, his nostrils sought and found the hint of roses and oranges.

"What are you doing here?" she asked.

That sweetly ambling voice of hers made him want to sit back and relax. "We need to talk."

"I'm busy," she said flatly, thumbing the face of her phone to check the time. "I have an interview." She started to move around him, but he held out his hand.

It was enough to stop her. She very pointedly held herself back from accidentally brushing his arm.

Her aversion stung.

"I have to catch a bus," she said stiffly.

Seeing her in this low-end building, using public transport, gave his conscience another yank. He had another reason for being here besides the possibility of pregnancy. He needed to know for sure. Was she really estranged from her father? Had he really crushed an innocent beneath his heel that day?

"I have your things in my car," he said, "I'll drive you wherever you need to go."

"Mom's pearls?" Her averted gaze flew to his, round and anxious. "Why didn't you bring them in?"

"I saw you through the window as I was getting out. I thought—" That she might somehow escape him if he didn't act fast to catch her here in the foyer. His actions had been pure reflex.

She figured out what he'd almost revealed. "We have nothing to say to each other, Roman," she said tonelessly. "Just go out and get them. I'd like them back."

"We do have to talk," he asserted firmly, watching her for signs of evasion. When she only gave a firm shake of her head, refusing to look at him, he reminded her, "I didn't use anything that day."

Her expression blanked before comprehension dawned in a dark flood of color. Her jaw fell open, appalled. "I'm not pregnant!" she cried.

Someone down the hall opened a door and peeked out.

Melodie was scarlet with embarrassed anger. Her dismayed blue eyes glared into his as she folded her arms defensively, mouth pouted in humiliation. "I'm not."

"Are you sure?" he challenged.

"Of course I am. But I'm stunned that you've tracked me down to ask. I assumed you'd been careless on purpose. When it comes to ruining a woman's life, leaving her with an unplanned pregnancy is about as effective as it gets."

That bludgeoned hard enough to knock him back a step.

"I wouldn't do that." He was deeply offended she would think him capable of such a coldhearted form of revenge. When she only lifted disinterested brows, he insisted, "I wouldn't. I know too well what it's like to *be* an unplanned baby. I'm here to take care of my child if I have one. Do I?"

"No," Melodie insisted, forcing herself to meet his gaze even though it was very hard. She was telling the truth, but she didn't want to see his sincerity or have empathy and understand him. She only wanted to put him and her grave error behind her.

But his being here, asking the question, affected her. She'd been relieved when things had cycled along as normal. Of course she'd been relieved. Yet a small part of her had suffered a wistful moment. A baby would have been a disaster, but it would have been family. Real family. The kind she could love.

Holding out a hand, she said, "Can you just give me my mother's necklace?"

"There's definitely no baby."

"Definitely."

He absorbed that with barely a twitch of his stoic expression before he jerked his head and held the door for her.

Dear Lord, he was handsome with those long, clean-shaven cheeks set off by his turned up collar, his mouth pursed in dismay, his short thick hair tossing in the bluster of wind that grabbed at them.

The fierce breeze yanked her bound hair and shot up her skirt to bite at her skin. She clenched her teeth and beelined for the limo at the curb.

He opened the back door himself. "What's the address of where you're going?"

"Don't do me any favors, Roman. I'll just take the necklace and go."

"You're refusing my help out of spite?"

"I'm protecting what's left of my self-respect." Her knees knocked as the blustering cold penetrated mercilessly. Teeth chattering, she held out her hand. "Pearls?"

"They're right there. Get in. I have more to say."

"To quote *you*, I don't *care*."

With an air of arrogant patience, he closed another button on his coat and set his back to the wind, adopting a stance of willingness to wait for the spring thaw.

"You won't just hand them to me. You're determined

to make me miss my job interview. Look around. Getting me fired did nothing to my father," she charged.

"I know that I misjudged you," he snapped back. "But your father and brother are on the attack against me. That's not up for dispute. It's reality. And it's not common knowledge that you've lived apart from them all these years. Given the way things looked in the funeral photos, it was an easy mistake to make."

"I know," she said with the same impatience. She could understand and almost forgive that part. She had plenty of unexpressed anger of her own toward her father and brother. "And I have no problem believing they stole from you."

His brows went up a smidgen. "Not many would take my word for it."

"Anton isn't capable of writing his own email, let alone launching a high-tech start-up. I've always wondered how he managed it." She smiled bitterly. "And I have a lot of experience with how low they can sink."

His gaze sharpened and she dropped her own, shielding herself, unprepared to let him delve into all the anguish and fury roiling inside her.

"So get in."

"No."

"For God's sake, why not?"

"Because I don't trust you!"

His head went back and his expression grew carved and stoic. "I'm not going to touch you. I didn't mean to sleep with you that day."

"Oh, that's funny," she choked, trying to end that topic before it went any further. She was mortified he'd brought it up.

"It's the truth," he shot back, his energy like a living thing that whipped and raced on the tail of the wind, lashing her with its force. He was tense. Very tense as he confronted her, as if he was willing her to believe him. It was weirdly fascinating.

She tore her gaze away, not wanting to get caught up in trying to decipher the truth from his lies. Not wanting to hear excuses and let down her guard. He'd already gotten past her defenses too easily, setting her back so she was as naked and defenseless as she'd been that day. It wasn't him she mistrusted, but herself.

She ought to be able to shut him out the way she had with her father and Anton. Roman meant nothing to her. Less than nothing. As bitter as she was toward her father and half brother, she went days, weeks even, without thinking of them, but no such luck with Roman. He was top of her mind every day, ambushing her with memories of kisses and caresses and wrenching pleasure.

She swallowed, not wanting the recollections to surface now.

Her blood warmed anyway. Her senses heightened, making her aware of his scent, masculine and sharp, beneath the sweet smell of rain and the comforting notes of damp wool. Clothing didn't make a man, but everything about his appearance amplified his stark masculinity. His cheekbones were proud and chiseled, his nose a blade, his lips twitching almost into a closed-mouth kiss as he prepared to speak.

"I slept with you in spite of who you are, not because of it," he said in a growl.

"Had a staggering crash in your standards, did you?" Insult blindsided her as she absorbed that he was saying she'd been willing and he had merely taken advantage. Any man would. "At least when I thought you seduced me for revenge, it was personal. I honestly thought I couldn't feel worse about that day. Thanks, Roman. You're a real guy."

"And you're twisting me into a far more vicious bastard than I am."

She stared at him, astonished. "You made *hatred* to me." The words swelled in her throat. She clenched her jaw, trying to hold back convulsive shivers, trying to hold on to control and not allow emotion to rise up and sting her eyes. "At least I had some respect for you that afternoon, before you started ruining my life."

"Would you get in the damned car?"

She realized people were walking by, staring. Overhearing.

She was freezing, and warm air radiated from the interior. With a sob of annoyed misery, she threw herself into the backscat.

He followed and slammed the door, adjusting the vents so hot gushes of air poured directly onto her.

She didn't thank him, even though her legs were stinging and her fingers were numb. She attacked the box with her name on it, spilling her mother's necklace into her lap. Picking it up, she pressed the treasured beads to her lips.

"I only meant to do to you what they did to me, which was cut short your career and leave you with bills to pay," Roman said.

She dropped her hands. "But you accidentally slept with me, even though you hated me," she charged, going hot again. Bristling with temper.

"Yes," he asserted, as if that proved some kind of point beyond the fact he was a conscienceless womanizer.

"To humiliate me," she confirmed in a jagged voice, looking over at him in time to see guilt flash across his expression before he controlled it.

"I thought you were throwing yourself at me for their purposes. It looked as if you were trying to trick me into letting you stay in my house. I let you come on to me so I could turn you down," he admitted.

"But you went through with it," she said, returning to that deep sense of bitterness that had burned through her with every step of her journey back to the hotel that day, as she'd absorbed that what had looked like a white knight had actually been the same blackened soul that the men in her family possessed. "How do people like you sleep at night? That's what I want to know."

"Do *not* lump me in with them, Melodie," he fired back, temper riled enough to darken his expression and press her into her seat. "Do you see them chasing you down the East Coast to ask about consequences? I am *not* just like them." His jaw worked. "I'll be the first to admit I'm not a good man, definitely not a great one, but I'm *not* as immoral as they are."

The way she'd set him on the same reprehensible shelf as the Gautier men ate at him. She could see it. That should have been more satisfying, but it just made her feel small.

"Sleeping with you just happened," he muttered.

"Because I threw myself at you," she provided, feeling the sting press forward from the backs of her eyes to blur her vision. "Because you couldn't resist me." *Spider arms. Freak.*

She narrowed her eyes, turning her face away as she willed Anton's voice to silence and willed her tears to dry before they squeezed past her lashes and fell.

"Yes."

She hated Roman in that moment. Really hated him. Because he sounded so begrudging as he said it. Not smooth and charming and manipulative. Resentful. He sounded as confounded by his reaction as she was by hers. That made him sound truthful even though she was convinced he had to be lying.

"I know I'm not beautiful. At best, I'm striking," she said, straining to keep emotion from her voice. "I'm certainly not the type who inspires lust, so give it a rest. You wanted to hurt me. Which you did."

"I'm not here to hurt you again," he ground out, flinching as though she'd slapped him. "I can't take back what I did. If I could…" he began tightly, emotions so compressed she couldn't read anything in his tone but intensity.

He *would* take it back? Her heart clenched in a surprisingly strong contraction of agony.

Of course she would take it back, too, she assured herself, even as their heights of pleasure danced through her consciousness, reminded her how rare and singular the experience had been. He'd ruined her for accepting anything less, if he wanted the truth, which left her feeling bleak and hopeless.

"You told me that day that you were attracted to me," he said.

"Don't throw that in my face," she cried, recoiling from being mocked.

"I was attracted, too. More than I knew how to handle. That's why I slept with you. Not out of revenge. Not to humiliate you."

She swallowed, wavering toward believing him, but it strained credulity. "It wasn't love at first sight, Roman. I saw the way you looked at me the day I arrived. You weren't interested."

"I didn't let my interest show. There's a difference."

She had to turn her nose to the window then, hope rising too quickly. Did she have no sense of self-preservation? Believing in him had only gotten her a giant helping of heartache the last time.

But he was very contained, not giving away much, very good at keeping his thoughts and feelings well hidden. Maybe he had been attracted.

Even if he had been, so what?

With a troubled sigh, she realized she was crushing the pearls in her clenched hands. Her fingers were warm enough to work now. She reached to close the strand around her throat.

Wool slid against leather and Roman was in her space, fingers brushing hers.

With an alarm that came more from a jolt of excitement than fear, she released the pearls and let him take over, angling herself so he could finish quickly. Her skin tightened all over her body as his knuckles brushed the tiny, upswept hairs at the back of her head. Beneath her layers of clothing her nipples tightened into sharp peaks and her blood grew hot, radiating heat outward to dispel any lingering chill for the rest of time.

The moment he was done she shifted away from his disturbing touch, adjusting the weight of the necklace so it felt right, and flashed a nervous glance his way.

He was watching her intently. "I felt it, too. There's something in our chemistry."

"I don't know what you're talking about," she dismissed with an unsettled shake of her head. If the traffic hadn't been so busy, she would have pushed out her side of the car. "I need to get to my job interview. Let me out."

"Don't start lying to me now, Melodie. Not when we're clearing the air." He didn't move.

Her heart began to pound with a trapped bird sort of panic. "Look," she said, tugging the hem of her skirt down her knee. Electricity seemed to crackle between them like fingers of lightning. "I know I gave you the impression I'm easy. I'm not. So don't start with your moves."

"Moves," he repeated on a dry chuckle. "Like how I seduced you that day? *You* kissed *me*."

"Don't remind me!" she cried.

"I will remind you," he said, leaning into her. "And I'll even be honest enough to admit I lied to you that day. I said it's always like that for me, but who has an encounter like that *ever* in their lifetime?"

Melodie shot her gaze to his. He was so close and disturbing. His brow was pulled into a perturbed line, his skin taut with challenge and something else. Discomfort, maybe, with how much he was admitting.

Between one breath and the next the shared memory of their wild coming together filled the tiny space behind these tinted windows.

She couldn't look away from his rain-forest eyes. He pinned her in place with nothing but a tiny shift of his attention to her mouth.

Her heart began to race and her blood felt as though it zigzagged in her veins. Her breasts flooded with heat, growing heavy and achy, the tips tight with reaction.

Desire clouded his irises.

A fog of longing smothered her consciousness, making sensible thought slippery and vague. She found herself looking at his mouth. In her dreams those lips plundered hers. She always woke with one question uppermost in her mind: Had it really been that good?

His lips parted as he came closer.

She opened with instinctive welcome.

They made contact and intense relief washed through her as a great thirst was finally slaked. His hand came to the side of her face, open and tender. She tilted into his touch, feeling moved and cherished as he cradled her head and gently but thoroughly devoured her.

She drew on him with greedy abandon, forgetting everything except that he filled a vast need in her. There were no words, just a craving that both ceased and grew as they locked mouths and touched tongues. His body closed in, pressed. He overwhelmed her as he wrapped his arms fully around her.

She moaned, pleasure blooming in her like a supernova. She instantly ached for more intimate contact with him.

His arms tightened, gathering her to draw her with him as he sat back, pulling her into his lap.

The shift was enough of a jolt to make her pull back

and realize where they were, how her knees had fallen on either side of his thighs, skirt riding up. She was losing all contact with reality. Again.

Then what?

"This can't happen," she gasped.

She pushed off him, throwing herself awkwardly onto the seat opposite and glaring back at him. She felt like a mouse that might have freed herself from the cat's mouth, but only until he wanted to clamp down on her again.

"Not here, no. Come to my hotel with me," he said, voice sandpapery and exquisitely inviting.

"For what?" she cried.

"Don't be dense," he growled. "We're an incredible combination. You can feel the power of it as well as I can."

"You've really perfected this technique of yours, haven't you?" she choked. "Listen, you might sleep with people you loathe, but I don't. I won't sleep with a man I hate."

He snapped his head back.

Her conscience prickled. She didn't hate him. There was too much empathy and understanding in her for such a heartless emotion.

"Well, that's that. Isn't it?" He thrust himself from the car, holding the door open for her.

Icy wind flew in to accost her, scraping her legs and stabbing through her clothes as she rose from the cozy interior to the ferocity of winter, entire body shaking, heart fragile.

"Goodbye, Roman," she said, feeling as if she was losing something as precious as her mother's pearls.

"Melodie."

Not goodbye, she noted, but his tone still sounded final and made her unutterably sad. Clutching the edges of her jacket closed, she walked to the bus stop on heavy feet.

CHAPTER SIX

ROMAN WENT BACK to his house in France where he could live in his own personal exile and ruminate, but despite only being here once, Melodie infused the place.

He never should have gone after her. If it hadn't been for the possibility of a baby, he wouldn't have, but there was no way he could have let a child of his grow up the way he had—not just poor and alone, but with a million questions and a million facets of rejection glittering into the furthest corners of its psyche. The one time he'd asked his mother about his father, she'd said, "He was a rich man who said he loved me, but I guess he didn't because he didn't come back."

He was a rich man, one who was very careful not to use those words and provoke false hope. He'd always hated his father for being a liar while secretly fearing he was just like the man: incapable of real love. He wasn't particularly likable. He knew that. Foster care had taught him to hold back, be cautious, not expect that he was anything but a burden to be tolerated. He came in too late with any sign of caring, long after he'd been written off as stunted. This was why he didn't pursue serious relationships with women or even have close friendships.

But he didn't usually provoke people to hatred. It maddened him that Melodie felt that way. He shouldn't have kissed her, he knew that, but the attraction between them had still been there. She'd responded to his touch.

Yet she reviled him too much to let things progress.

While he could think of nothing but touching her again. Grazing the warmth of her neck with his fingertips had been the height of eroticism. Kissing her again had inflamed him.

The fact that she was driving him insane, mentally and physically, told him it was time to cut ties altogether. It was time to forget her and move on with his life.

Melodie had always read her horoscope, trusted in karma and hoped fate really did have a plan for her. For the sake of her sanity she clung to the belief that good things happened to good people if they stuck in there long enough. The Gautier men were masters of cynicism, but she was different. And she wouldn't crumble under the weight of the dark side like her mother had, taking the first path out of life that was offered. She would fight and prevail.

Then Roman Killian had happened.

He'd not only shown her that she couldn't trust her own instincts and judgment, he'd provoked bitterness and pessimism in her. A depressing attitude lingered in her long after her encounter with him in his limo, an aimless feeling of "what's the point?"

That wasn't like her, but she couldn't seem to shake the mood. Her only hope was that fulfilling her mother's wish for her remains to float down the Seine would help her find closure and move on. Accomplishing that was the reason she had sold her soul and taken the job campaigning with Trenton Sadler.

And, since fate had a sense of humor, that seemed to demand she face Roman Killian again.

As coincidences went, winding up at a New York gala he was attending was a kick in the teeth from the karmic gods, but what had she done to make the planets align against her so maliciously?

Maybe it was just a fluke. She *was* traveling in higher circles these days, literally traveling, finally seeing New York if only from a hotel window. Her new employer was actively seeking corporate introductions, happy to be seen hobnobbing with lobbyists and special-interest groups.

He was exactly like her father, and she'd made her deal with Trenton Sadler like a blues guitarist shaking hands with Satan at the crossroads. He didn't know she was a senator's daughter. No, he thought she was simply a surprise talent he'd rescued from a temp agency, one who'd dabbled in catering and event planning. But Melodie was pulling out every maneuver she'd ever learned at Daddy's knee. Trenton loved her for it.

She didn't care for him at all, hated the work because it had everything to do with political-party advancement and nothing to do with the needs of the people, but she was good at it, and the compensation was more than a livable wage. And Trenton had promised her a bonus if he got the nomination he was after. It would be enough to square up her line of credit and fund her trip to Paris.

That was the only reason she was living out of a suitcase along with the rest of Trenton's handlers, renting black strapless evening gowns and pressing palms while conjuring a vapid smile. Tonight she'd lost track of whether they were buying or selling, whether this was a fund-raiser or a charity auction or a grand opening. All she knew was that she was in another hotel ballroom. She felt as if she'd come full circle, accomplishing nothing with her life, when she glanced toward the entrance and saw *him*.

Her heart gave a lurch.

Roman Killian had the uncanny ability to make whatever he wore fall into the background so all she noticed was the magnificence of the man. His head was tilted down to a beautiful blonde by his side, but with a disconcerting suddenness he jerked his head up and scanned the room.

Melodie watched with morbid fascination, thinking she was imagining what she was seeing, but as she watched, Roman cataloged the crowd like a robotic laser shone from his eyes. The blonde continued speaking, but he didn't seem to notice. His visage slowly rotated toward Melodie, as though he was computing every face in the room until—

He stopped when he spotted her.

She was almost knocked back a step. All of her froze except her pulse, which galloped like a spooked horse, kicking and squealing. His hair was extra rakish tonight, suggesting that the woman's fingers had ruffled it. His jaw looked hard and polished. His expression was completely unreadable as he kept his gaze fixed on her.

"Who is that?" Trenton asked beside her, rattling her out of her stasis.

"Roman Killian." Her throat was dry. Her entire being went numb as Roman flicked his gaze to Trenton and came back to her before he turned his attention to the blonde, his expression inscrutable.

"Tech-Sec Industries?" Trenton asked, forcing Melodie to bring her mind back from a limo and a kiss that had been every bit as profound and memorable as the ones in France and twice as much of a letdown afterward. "Why didn't you tell me you had a connection like that?"

"I don't," she said huskily. "We've only met once. Twice." *Three times.* "We're not friends," she assured him.

"Sure about that?" Trenton asked, giving her the kind of male once-over he'd started sending her way this trip. She had watched him flirt openly with more than one impressionable young supporter in his office, despite having a wife who kept the home fires burning. He hadn't gone out of his way to hit on Melodie, though, preferring to bark orders for coffee and sandwiches in her direction. Being the only female traveling with the group seemed to have elevated her to a target, however.

"I'm sure," she affirmed, recalling her last words to Roman, which had been most unfriendly. She tried to clear the catch from her throat as she added, "I should leave, or I might become a liability."

"No," he said with a thoughtful glance at the way Roman had joined a group near the bar, but had positioned himself so Melodie was in his line of sight. "Introduce us. Be as nice as you have to be to get him on my side. I want his support."

We don't always get what we want, Melodie wanted to say.

"He wasn't on the list," she reminded him. Mrs. Sadler had stayed home for this whirlwind junket. The rest of the team had stayed in their rooms and Melodie was standing in as Trenton's date, something he seemed to think gave him the right to hands-on access. She'd been finding ways to sidestep, but she had her assignment when it came to ensuring the right connections were made. Roman Killian wasn't one of the names in the room they had to touch base with, though.

In fact, if she'd known he'd be attending, she would have wormed her way out of this evening altogether. Mentally reviewing the guest list, she recalled a Swedish actress had been on it. Roman must be her plus one. Why his being involved with someone should cause a pinch near her heart, Melodie had no idea, but she didn't want to get close enough to see how deep his involvement with the stacked blonde went.

Trenton didn't care about her needs, though. "Introduce us," he repeated firmly.

Paris, she thought.

"If you like." She gathered her courage and found a stiff smile.

It took time to work through the crowded ballroom. They had to stop midway to listen to a speech about the refurbishment of this iconic hotel, one of New York's first skyscrapers. Applause happened, balloons fell, dancing started.

Melodie tried to pretend she wasn't in an intricate waltz with Roman, one in which she took two steps forward and sidestepped one. She was aware of his every shift and turn as he and his date worked the room. When he took the actress to the dance floor, Melodie told herself she only noticed because he was Trenton's quarry. They were gaining on him.

He came off the dance floor feet away from where she stood with Trenton, practically an invitation to approach. The tray of champagne appeared to have been their goal. Roman took two and turned his back on Melodie as he handed a flute to the blonde, but the opportunity was at hand.

Melodie felt his nearness like the heat off a blaze. Anticipation began to buzz in her. She neutralized her nerves by setting a light touch on Trenton's arm to break into his current conversation.

"I believe our opening has arrived," she told him, smiling a goodbye at the navy general and his wife as Trenton covered her hand, insisting she maintain the contact while they crossed the small distance to where Roman and his girlfriend were sipping their drinks.

Roman looked at her, and it was the same sweep of her feet out from under her as ever. All the air seemed to leave her body under the impact of his cool, green gaze and she had to gather her composure just to speak.

"Mr. Killian. What a surprise to bump into you here. I don't think you know Trenton Sadler—"

"I've seen the ads," Roman said, flicking a cynical twitch of his lips at Trenton as they shook hands. "This is Greta Sorensen."

"I've seen some of your films. I love romantic comedies," Melodie said, sincere for the first time all evening.

"I'm filming one now. That's why I'm here in New York," Greta said in her prettily accented English.

"And she has to be at work very early tomorrow morning," Roman said. "So we were just leaving. Good night." It was quite a snub, one that made Greta's eyes widen slightly before she turned it into a smoky look of anticipation aimed straight at Roman.

"I'll assume that brush-off was meant for you, not me," Trenton said tightly as Roman steered Greta toward the exit.

"I told you we weren't friends." Melodie reeled from the rebuff, her entire body stinging as though she'd been lashed front and back. Something in her ought to have been worried about how this would impact her job, but all she could think was that the encounter had made her incredibly sad. Especially if he was in a rush to make love to his date before she got her unnecessary beauty sleep. Lucky Greta.

"You didn't exactly try to kiss and make up, did you?" Trenton charged.

Ah, the temperament of the politically hungry. Melodie ignored his tone, swallowed back a disturbing thickness in her throat and adopted her own implacable smile as she nudged Trenton toward a paunchy older gentleman. Work. Paris. She would not speculate on what Roman was doing with that Swedish sex kitten.

Nor would she wonder what her life would look like right now if she'd allowed Roman to take her back to his hotel room that day four months ago. Had she been tempted? On a physical level, absolutely. Even now, she regularly woke up damp with perspiration, deeply aroused, remnants of sexually explicit dreams lingering behind her clenched eyes.

Why did he have to torture her this way?

A man who could set aside revulsion toward a woman and bed her anyway was obviously incapable of the sort of love and respect she had always wanted. He'd battered her heart so thoroughly she doubted she'd ever recover.

Which made her furious with him all over again.

Firm hands descended on her waist from behind.

She gasped under a jolt of electricity, nerve endings flaring hotly, immediately aware who was touching her. She covered his hands, trying to remove them, but he only held on more possessively.

Trenton broke off midspiel and glanced at her, brows going up as he recognized who stood behind her. "I thought you were taking your date home?" he said.

"She's staying on the eleventh floor. Dance with me, Melodie."

No. She couldn't breathe to speak.

"Good idea," Trenton said, piercing her with a significant "be nice" look.

Numbly she let Roman guide her onto the dance floor. Actually, she wasn't numb. She was so sensitive every touch and smell and sound overwhelmed her. She couldn't pick out the beat in the music or tell whether his hands were hot or her skin was flushing in reaction to his hold on her. Her throat hurt where her pulse thrummed. Her limbs felt clumsy as she set one hand on his shoulder and the other hand in his.

"Why—?" she tried, but her voice didn't want to work. She wasn't sure what she was asking anyway. So many questions crowded up from the hollow space between her knotted stomach and her tight lungs she couldn't make sense of a single one.

"Are you sleeping with him?" he asked with seeming disinterest. "He's married, you know."

She snorted, disdainful words choking past the locked

gate of her collarbone. "I'm aware, and no. He's my boss. What happened to Greta? Turn you down?"

"I don't sleep with clients, but she wanted to make an appearance." His touch on her changed, fingers closing more firmly over hers. His hand weighed more heavily at her waist. A hint of dry humor glinted in his eye. "Now that we've got that out of the way…"

"I don't care," she tried, but came up against her own dishonesty as quickly as his smirk flashed and disappeared.

"No. Of course not. You hate me. Why are you dancing with mc, thcn?"

"I was told to be nice to you." Offering a lethal mimic of Greta's smoky look, she warned, "Do *not* get me fired, Roman. I *will* kill you."

"He's a sycophant."

"So am I," she retorted, squirming inwardly at being caught out as one of Trenton's minions. "It pays the bills."

Roman's mouth tightened briefly before he allowed, "You're good at working a room. I've been watching you."

Melodie tingled with awareness at the idea of his watching her, covering her reaction with a blasé "Mom always needed a wing woman at these sorts of things. When it was her turn to host, I made all the arrangements. Ingrid's wedding really would have come off beautifully under my hand, you know. How are the arrangements coming along?"

"I have no idea. She's training her replacement and that's enough comedy for my tastes."

"Because weddings are a joke? Falling in love is for the weak and pathetic? I'm beginning to agree with you, Roman. Which makes me hate you all the more," she added with a quiet burst of ferocity.

He spun her off the dance floor and behind a mirrored column.

"I tried to apologize to you that day," he reminded hotly.

"You tried to pick me up," she threw back, scraped raw all over again.

Four months had passed since their last meeting and Roman had managed to convince himself he'd forgotten her. The moment he had entered the room, however, a preternatural sense had sparked awake in him. He'd known she was here.

Then he'd spied her, toffee hair swept up to reveal her long neck and those deliciously modest pearls. Her shoulders were bared by her dress. The rest of her gown had hardly impacted upon him as he'd taken in the statue-still bust her head and shoulders made staring back at him.

She still hated him, he'd seen immediately, judging by her lack of a smile.

Then he'd seen her date touch her arm and something had snapped awake in him, an emotion that was blade sharp and ferocious. He suspected it was jealousy, because for a moment he'd been blind. All the hairs had lifted on his body and his blood had pumped in anticipation as he had prepared to shove through the crowd to get to her.

Sense had prevailed, albeit very weakly. He hadn't been able to dump his date fast enough and get back to Melodie once she'd opened the borders and spoken to him. Now her scent filled his nostrils and his muscles twitched to clamp his arms around her. He was primed to throw her over his shoulder and steal her from the room while fighting off rivals.

He was damned close to doing so. The bitter look she gave him was filled with acid and ate away at what control he had.

"Do you think I wouldn't control this if I could? That I don't hate *you* for affecting *me* like this?" He threw the words at her.

Her head flung back as if he'd slapped her.

"No, it doesn't feel very good, does it?" he gritted out, skin threatening to split under the pressure of containing himself. "It's not me doing this to you, Melodie. It's *us*. I'm this close to having you against this damned wall with the entire room watching. It's that powerful."

"Even though you hate me." She turned her face to the side, eyes glistening.

"What do you want me to say? That I love you?" The word caught like a barbed hook on the way out, snagging in his chest and the back of his throat. It wasn't a word he even understood beyond its bastardized use. *I love this car. I love crème brulée.*

"I wouldn't believe you if you did, but I want the man I sleep with to say it," she said with a break of anguish in her voice. "I want to feel it. It's the only thing that's kept me going all those years, believing I'd make better choices with men than my mother did. I'm so lonely I want to cry, but I can't bring myself to believe any of you anymore." Her lips trembled. "You *broke* me, Roman. That's why I hate you."

He sucked in a breath that felt like razor blades.

"I hate being this person. I hate being skeptical and negative," she went on, skimming trembling fingertips beneath her eyes. "I hate using words like *hate*." She sent a quick, desperate glance toward the exit. "I need to go to the ladies' room."

Because she was falling apart.

He thought he might. *Hell*.

Catching her arm, he used his height and confidence to muscle through the crowd to where a bellman was checking names at the door. "You have something for me. Roman Killian."

"Of course. Right here, sir." The bellman handed over a small folder with a number on the inside cover. It contained Roman's room key and the credit card he'd handed to a member of staff on his way back into the ballroom after dropping off Greta with a handshake.

He hadn't intended to book a room here until he'd seen Melodie.

Melodie gave a muted sniff and turned toward a sign pointing out the facilities, but he drew her across the atrium toward the elevators.

"I can't leave," she said, accepting Roman's handkerchief as he hustled her along. Then she paused to lean into her smudged reflection in an etched panel. "Actually, I should go to my room to fix my makeup."

The elevator doors opened and he pressed her into the car.

"Six," she said.

He ignored that and pressed the P.

"Roman—" She started to poke 6.

He stopped her. "We're going to talk, Melodie. Clear the air once and for all."

"There's no point," she insisted, voice husky and fatalistic. "You're right. We do goad each other and bring out the worst. That means we should stay as far away from each other as possible."

Her words spiked into him, making him fearful to draw breath, knowing it would burn. "Do you really think that?"

A rush of emotion welled in her eyes and made her clamp her lips together. She dropped her gaze.

"I didn't listen to you that first day. We might not have damaged each other so badly if I had. This time we get it all on the table. Neither of us can move forward until we do."

"I damaged you?" she asked with disbelief. "How?"

"You made me question whether I'm a worthy human being."

CHAPTER SEVEN

MELODIE FLINCHED AT being called out for hurting him, astonished that she could.

And disturbed. It meant they really were bad for each other. So how could she drop her anger and embrace the idea they could sort things out? Anger was safe. Listening and understanding would only make her feel guilty and vulnerable. Trusting Roman would mean abandoning her defensive animosity, and that scared her. It would leave her with nothing to hold him off.

He still scared her, she admitted privately. Still caused a reaction in her that was stronger than logic. Whether it was fury or passion, she'd never dealt with such intense feelings. The closest she'd come had been the fire that had burned inside her while fighting with her father over her mother's care. Those emotions had made sense, though. They'd been born of deep loyalty and love…

She cut short looking for similarities. Roman was a stranger. They'd only met a handful of times, and even she, with her Pollyanna ideals, suspected love at first sight was a myth. If it did exist it wouldn't feel like this. As if a man she barely knew was a god with the power to smite her in a blink.

As they entered the penthouse, he went to the bar while she took in the well-appointed suite with its view of the New York skyline, its Old English furniture and its softly glowing vintage lamps draped in shimmering crystal beads.

"Scotch? Or wine?" he asked, holding up a bottle.

"I can't stay long." She glanced at the time on her phone, ignored a text from one of the aides asking how things were going and dropped the device back into her clutch, sighing heavily. "What is there to say anyway? I was feeling very low about my mother's death when we met. I wanted to meet someone, to feel alive. I let myself think there was more potential between us than there was. I shouldn't have slept with you, but I did. It gave you the wrong impression about how I conduct myself."

He brought her a glass of white wine, the glass frosted by the chill of the liquid. His expression was cool and unreadable. She sipped, wetting her dry tongue and soothing her burning throat, trying to collect herself while the strange energy that emanated off him took her apart at the seams.

"Did you hear me that day in the car? I didn't make *hatred* to you. There was nothing in my mind at that moment except the pleasure we were giving each other."

"Don't," she said, brushing a wisp of hair behind her ear and using the motion to hide her flinch of self-consciousness.

"We have to be frank. I don't like it any more than you do." He brought his glass of neat scotch up to his lips but paused and lowered it again. "I don't chase women for sport, Melodie. It's important to me that you believe that. I'm lousy in a relationship, but not because I treat women like sex providers. If I hadn't had a reason to kick you out that day, you would have been in my bed until *you* tired of *me*."

"Does that happen?" she asked with a faint attempt at levity. It was supposed to be a swipe at the man she assumed him to be: a gorgeous playboy with enough money to hold any woman's interest.

"I'm emotionally inaccessible," he said with a pained

smile, as if it was a tragic but proved fact. "And the sex has never been like it is with us." He spoke as though it was something happening in the now, and indicated the invisible strands that pulled her toward him and, if he was to be believed, drew him just as inexorably.

She shifted away from the disturbing aura of sexual tension that grew between them so easily, feeling terribly weak. She would understand this gross sense of helplessness if she had given her heart to him. As a child yearning for love and approval from Garner and Anton, she'd walked around as spineless as her mother, taking each slight to heart. Eventually, living in the real world, she'd suffered fewer attacks, and most of them from people she cared little about. Her inner defenses had rallied and strengthened.

Now, after a handful of encounters with Roman, a man who should mean nothing to her, she was more emotionally sensitive than ever, responding to every word he said as if it was her own inner voice. It was disconcerting.

She eyed him, unsettled by his talk of feeling the same irrevocable pull. "I don't understand how it can be like this if we don't love each other."

"I've never understood how love enters into sex at all." He tilted his glass to watch the liquid move in the square bottom of his glass. "I've always thought pleasure was the point. Don't look like that," he chided gently, glancing up to catch what was probably a wounded expression on her face. "I didn't say that to mock you. I'm being honest."

She ducked her head. "It still hurts. You didn't even think I was attractive, Roman. It wasn't until the second day that you started to act as though you were interested, and that was after you knew who I was."

"I told you in Virginia, just because I didn't let it show doesn't mean I wasn't attracted. I'm not interested in serious relationships, Melodie. By that I mean marriage, kids, a lifetime commitment… I'm not cut out for that. You looked like the kind who is. So you're right, at that first meeting I made sure to keep my interest hidden to avoid going down a dead-end road. Then you smiled for the pictures and…" He frowned, took a sip of scotch and curled his lip in self-deprecation. "The truth is I was captivated. I couldn't hide how I was reacting when you came back the next day. I stopped trying. You're very beautiful."

She shook her head, not comfortable hearing that ever, but especially from him. Especially now. "Roman, I'm trying to believe you. I need to make sense of all this, but we have to be honest if—"

"Your mother was in magazines," he cut in with a baffled look. "You resemble her. How could you not know how pretty you are?"

Anton. She didn't say it. She wanted to be completely over him and his ugly criticisms.

"Mom was always described as *unusual* or *arresting*. She was just really emotive in front of a camera, unable to hide what she was feeling."

"And you're the same. Your true self comes through, and that woman is lovely, Melodie. I should have paid attention to that, not the fact that you happen to share the name Gautier," he added in a mutter aimed at the bottom of his glass.

She took a few swift footsteps away. He made her feel positively defenseless. She did everything in her power not to react, even though she wanted to flinch, while her pulse tripped in alarm and insecurity attacked her. She had worked so hard to get over all the self-doubts instilled by her upbringing. If there was any benefit to her mother's hospitalization, it had been the secondhand counseling she'd received. She may not have battled the same physiological depression her mother had fought, but her early years had been exactly the same steady erosion of her self-esteem that her mother had faced.

Now Roman was saying he could see past all the small shields she'd managed to assemble for herself. It was terrifying. She stood in silence, trying to pretend he held no such power while she waited to see where and how he'd use his power to advantage.

"I don't *want* the ability to hurt you, Melodie," he said finally. "I'm emotionally detached by conscious decision, but I can't stay indifferent around you. *You*," he said with a significant tone. "No one else gets under my skin this way."

She almost found a shred of humor in his vexed tone. She could relate. The truth was she didn't want the power to hurt him, either.

"I don't understand why we're like this," she said. "We don't *know* each other."

"Don't we?" He set down his drink and pushed his bunched fists into his pockets. His shoulders went back and his profile was a sharp silhouette against the black windows. "Who holds a woman's ashes hostage so her daughter has to put her grief on display? It's as bad as stealing a young man's only hope for a future by threatening to expose his one mistake in the past."

Melodie swallowed, acknowledging that he probably did understand her at a very deep level. "Did Anton contribute *anything* to that software program that built his fortune?"

"His name." Roman's expression lost its warmth, hardening. "He was doing me the favor of attaching himself to it. I was desperate enough to give up fifty percent for that. After a sound beating, I agreed to a hundred."

Melodie gasped, feeling his words like a wrecking ball hitting her chest. But she supposed any man who could shake a woman until she begged for mercy could beat a man to a pulp.

"After Mom's funeral they were never going to be in

my life again. The job with Ingrid was a fresh start, finally a potential career. I couldn't have traveled for work
while Mom was alive. She needed to see me every day. We
needed each other," she corrected, setting down her own
glass and purse on a side table to hug herself.

"Dad always had final say in her care, so he was always this dark presence that kept me on edge. Then, finally, even though it was only her ashes, she *was* in my
care. I saw myself drawing a line under my childhood
but..." She shrugged, accosted by vulnerability again,
but it wasn't as hard this time. She was beginning to
feel safe making her confession to him. "You were supposed to be the redemption, Roman. You were supposed
to prove that not all men are the same. You let me down.
You proved that they can still hurt me. That all the bru-
tality and ugliness they put into the world is still able to
bounce back and hit me."

"Melodie, I didn't *know*."

"I know," she acknowledged with a jerky nod. "Anton
has a daughter out there from a college girlfriend. I check
in on her, send her money sometimes. He doesn't care.
You cared enough to show up and ask if you had a baby
on the way. I knew that day in the limo that you weren't
really like them. I just..."

"Still hate me."

"I'm trying to, Roman. If I don't, then you'll—"

"What?" he prompted quickly, demeanor changing.

He knew. She blushed and had to look away.

A muted noise sounded, and they both looked to the
clutch where she'd set it next to her glass. Her mobile vi-
brated inside it.

"Trenton is wondering where I am," she guessed, then
made a face, feeling as though she was with a friend after
all, she supposed, because she found herself saying a very

uncharitable, "I should text back that I'm *being nice* to you."

The banked sexual awareness between them flared like the catch of a match.

"That wasn't—" she hurried to say.

"I know." He sounded as though he was laughing at her, making her shoot a scowl his direction. "I'm not going to make another unwelcome pass, Melodie. No matter how much I want to."

Which was a pass in itself, she noted drily, but managed to say, "Good." Even though she was suddenly reluctant to accept that. Her mind was expanding with one ballooning thought. What would it be like now, when they'd set aside the misjudgments and animosity?

"I should go," she said briskly. Before she lost her mind.

"I'll walk you down."

"You don't have to." She picked up her clutch and headed toward the door.

He pocketed his room key off the bar and followed her. "Better if we both reappear without looking flushed and disheveled."

"Right." Flushed. Disheveled. Skin damp and whole body tingling in the aftermath of orgasm. That would be bad. "Yes," she affirmed. "You're probably right."

"Only probably? Don't give me an opening, Melodie. I will take it," he said.

They stood at the door, his hand on the latch, his white shirt and black jacket filling her vision.

"An opening for what?" She was playing dumb, not like her at all.

His mouth lifted at one corner, knowing. "I said I wouldn't make an unwelcome pass," he said, then touched her chin, gently forcing her to tilt up her face until she couldn't avoid his eyes. "If this is not welcome, say so now."

His touch was bringing her to life in ways she had thought were manifestations of an overactive imagination.

"I keep wondering—"

He covered her mouth and she knew. They were every bit as volatile as before. They stepped into the kiss with synchronicity, her arms going over his shoulders, his hands sliding to her lower back, pulling her hips into his. In heels she was eye level with his mouth, and they both moaned with pleasure at how perfectly they fit together.

The buzz sounded again from inside her purse.

They broke away.

She threw the clutch toward the sofa, missing. It hit the floor and slid while they stepped into tight contact again, lips meeting without hesitation or clumsiness. Her same distant thoughts of how and why penetrated, but she honestly didn't care. *He* was the man who did this to her. She couldn't turn away now that it had started. And there was no evidence of his trying to slow things down as his fingertips dug into her buttocks and he rotated to press her into the door.

Oh, the weight of him felt good!

Pushing into his thighs with her own, she incited where he was already hard.

He ground back, making a growling noise as he drew back just enough to smooth the fine hairs from her neck, then nipped and nibbled his way to her bare shoulder. The action was both tender and feral, as though he was asserting his dominance but with gentle care, demanding her capitulation in the exposure of her throat to him, rewarding her with caresses that trickled delicious fire through her whole body.

Threading fingers into his hair, she moaned his name, helpless to the onslaught of pleasure. Weak against the masculine power that didn't need muscle to overwhelm her.

"Feel what you're doing to me," he said, lifting his head

and dragging her hand to his neck. Beneath her palm his artery pulsed in hard, rapid pumps.

"Mine's going to explode, too," she said, drawing his hand to her chest, where her heart raced in such a rapid tattoo it alarmed her.

He slid his palm lower, cupping her breast, watching as he plumped the swell and circled the tip with his thumb, nipple tight and straining against silk.

Showers of delight glittered through her. She slid her hand to the back of his head and urged him to kiss her again.

He did, once, hard, then lifted his head. "I want to do it right." He clasped her hand, drew it from his hair so he could kiss her wrist. "I want to take our time and do it because we make each other feel so damned good. Stay with me."

It meant trusting him. Trusting that afterward he wouldn't throw her out and ruin her life.

Her stupid purse hummed, making her look past his shoulder with an anguished noise. When she tried to step away from him, he resisted letting her go. For one long second his muscles locked in refusal. Then he sucked in a breath and stepped back, hands up with frustrated surrender, shoulders hitting the wall next to the door as he accepted her rejection with a stoic face and a knock of his head into the wall behind him.

Paris, she thought. And, *Be nice*.

Looking back at Roman, at the way he'd lowered his eyelids to hide his thoughts but couldn't disguise the way his mouth had gone flat with dismay, she shrugged off doubts and skepticism. All she could think was *I want him*.

She walked over to kick her purse so it skittered under the sofa, then looked over her shoulder at him.

He came off the wall, alert.

Swallowing, she reached behind to begin lowering the zipper on her dress.

As it loosened across her bust, his breath hissed and his chest swelled. He came across to help.

She wanted to smile, but her gown puddled on the floor around her spiked heels. She hesitated, wearing only her bra and thong underpants, the vulnerability of the moment striking her with a sudden chill.

The way he looked at her bolstered her courage, though. His gaze ate her up while he shed his jacket, then pulled at his bow tie.

"Condom?" she managed to ask, trying to hang on to some shred of sense.

His expression blanked, hinted at panic, then he reached to pick up his jacket and swiftly went through the pockets, coming up with his wallet. Showing her the two foil packets he removed, he pushed them into his pants' pocket, dropped his jacket and chinned toward the opposite side of the room.

"Bedroom," he said in a graveled husk. "Or I'll have you over the back of this sofa. You make me insane, Melodie."

Yet he looked completely in control. It strained her trust, made her wonder for a bleak second if she was being reckless again. But the idea that she might have some kind of ability to provoke him was incredibly exciting.

She let her hips roll in a wicked sway as she walked ahead of him, providing what she supposed was a lurid view of her buttocks atop her long legs, but the thought made her feel sexy and desirable for the first time. With another twist of her arms behind her, she shed her bra as she went, leaving it on the floor, not turning around, smiling at the idea of teasing him.

"You're enjoying this," he accused, not sounding the least bit displeased as he came up behind her next to the bed and caught her back against him, one firm, confident hand capturing her breast as if he owned it.

It was both comforting and deeply provoking, especially when he gave her breast a firm caress and nearly buckled her knees with the catch of her nipple in a light pinch. She leaned into him weakly, legs shaking as he fondled more deliberately, playing with her nipple until she had to cover his hand to slow him down. It was getting too intense too quickly.

"Roman," she whispered, part protest, part plea.

"I want it to be so good for you that you know without a doubt that it's only about this, Melodie." His other hand slid to the front of her lace undies, fingertips slipping under without hesitation, cupping, massaging, working with gentle but insistent pressure to part and find her slick center.

Gasping, she wriggled back from his hot touch only to feel the thick ridge of his erection against her buttocks. She stilled with surprise.

"Yes, you're arousing me as much as I'm arousing you." His caress became deliberate, flagrant, pressing her into the thrust of his clothed hips against her backside as he drove her relentlessly toward orgasm.

Her head fell back against his shoulder while he took full advantage of her capitulation, biting the side of her neck.

"I want us to be together," she gasped, trying to still his hands on her, growing completely overwhelmed.

He lifted his mouth from sucking a mark onto her neck and said, "We will be. I'm going to lose it any second." His voice grated roughly, as stimulating as his touch. "Look," he said, shifting her slightly and there they were, caught in flagrante delicto in the mirror, his hands possessing her, his expression over her shoulder so filled with masculine intent she would have been alarmed, except then he strummed her again.

And told her how sexy she was, how badly he wanted her, how this was only the first of many so let him watch. Give him this because he needed to see he could make her feel good—

She cried out, embarrassed by the sight of herself losing control, so weakened by the buffet of climax she was wholly dependent on his support as he made it play out for her in lingering strokes that caused pulses of fading delight.

When she hung in his arms, he pressed hot, dry kisses and sexy compliments to her damp temple, finally turning her into his embrace so he could kiss her properly.

She belonged to him then. He utterly and completely owned her, and she didn't care. If misgivings surfaced, she brushed them away before she could identify them, too busy cradling his face so she could kiss him, telling him with her lips and body how incredible he made her feel.

He was hard, so hard all over. Absolutely primed with arousal, chest like sun-warmed bronze as she opened his shirt and caressed his hot, hard muscles. When she kissed her way across his chest, lightly brushing his beaded nipples with her fingertips, he threw back his head and groaned at the ceiling.

His reaction wasn't fake. What man as contained as he was would let her see the blind passion in his gaze as he cupped her cheeks and kissed the life out of her? What man that aroused would strip them both, then take his time pressing her to the bed?

What man wanting only to use a woman for his pleasure would kiss his way past her navel and ensure she was as ready as he was?

Sweeping her arms as though she was making angels in the satin sheets, she encouraged him with lusty moans, abandoning herself to the heaven of his tantalizing play. "Roman, I'm so close," she gasped.

He turned his mouth into her thigh, biting the twitching muscle there, drunk on her scent and taste, wishing he could hold out to finish her like this and arouse her again, but wanting her with him when he lost it inside her.

With a growl of strained control he slid up the silken length of her, pausing for light bites of her gorgeous breasts, eyes nearly rolling into the back of his skull as she framed his hips with her bent knees, offering herself. It was all he could do to fumble a condom into place.

The barest few words could be found in the miasma of his consciousness—*heat, softness, roses, citrus, wet, welcome. Melodie.*

She arched as he entered her, taking all of him in one slick thrust that sent a streak of sensation down his spine, flexing his shoulders and yanking his stomach muscles into a hot knot of masculine energy. His thoughts grew even more base. *Thrust, own.* She panted and clutched at him, opened her mouth to his kiss and licked at his tongue without inhibition.

The animal in him took over, protective enough to ensure he didn't hurt her, but driven by instinct to imprint himself indelibly. He returned to her again and again, his tension and level of stimulation so high he was blind and deaf to everything but her wordless expressions of yearning and need. He wanted everything she was. *Everything.*

"Give it to me. All of it," he ground out, needing her complete surrender to passion before he could give in to it himself.

Tossing her head, she cried out jaggedly, trembling beneath him, nails scraping down his upper arms as she bucked. Then it happened for her. He felt her release and his own struck like a hammer. He drove into her pulsing center and held himself there as they both were clenched in the paroxysm of orgasm.

Time stood still. Nothing mattered except this pleasure. No one existed but him and Melodie and this state of ecstasy.

Roman rolled away, forcing Melodie back to awareness of the room, how intimate they'd just been, that she was supposed to be working...

She covered her eyes with her forearm, not ready to face any of it.

The ring of the phone on the bedside table jarred into the silence. Roman came up on his elbow, damp skin brushing hers as he leaned across her, lifted the receiver and promptly dropped it back into its cradle.

Melodie peeked at him from under her arm. "Booty call from your Swedish friend?"

"For you, I imagine. I only booked the room an hour ago. No one I know would think to look for me here." Continuing to loom over her, he slid his leg across hers, pinning her erotically to the mattress as he picked up the receiver again and punched a number before bringing it to his ear. "Put my phone on Do Not Disturb," he ordered, then lowered the phone to ask Melodie, "Do you want anything?"

"I should go," she said, shifting restlessly under the weight of his leg.

Holding eye contact with her, he said into the phone, "We'll need a pair of overnight kits, toothbrushes and—" He paused to listen, then said, "Perfect. Thank you." He hung up. "The drawer in the bathroom likely has everything a couple might need, including more condoms."

"They said that?"

"It was implied."

"Did *I* imply that we needed more? Because I think I said I should go."

"Exactly. *Should.* Not that you were intending to."

"I begin to see why women tire of *you*," she said in a pert undertone. "Apparently you don't tire at all."

His grin flashed as he settled more of his weight on her and began searching her hair for pins. "Look, I'm no expert, but I'm thinking this hairdo of yours is *not* going back to the ballroom. So you might as well stay."

She should have taken her own hair apart, but instead she turned her head on the pillow to allow him to find the rest of the pins while she played delicate fingers across his collarbone and down to his biceps, where he braced himself on his forearm.

This was nice, she thought. It was the sort of sweet moment that *should* happen after lovemaking. If only…

"Why the sigh?" he asked, making her aware she'd released one. The last of her hairpins went onto the night table and he slid lower so they were eye to eye. "Regrets?" His tone held a fresh note of reserve.

"No," she said halfheartedly, then more sincerely, "No, this was…" Nice? Hardly. It had been basic and regressive. The blatant way he'd watched her come apart in the mirror, then devoted himself to her pleasure before stamping her with guttural thrusts rushed back at her. The burn of a self-conscious flush crept into her throat and face. "I'm embarrassed, if you want the truth. I don't fall into bed with men. I don't behave like this at all. Ever."

"Except with me," he said, as though making the statement of a closing argument.

"Except with you," she agreed softly, shifting her head so she felt his forearm under her cheek and had her lips against the smooth skin inside his biceps. He tasted faintly salty against her openmouthed kiss and smelled dark and masculine as she drew another fatalistic sigh.

"I'm not intuitive, Melodie, but you don't sound happy about that."

"Because even if I stay the night, I still have to leave in the morning. I'll never feel like this again and that's depressing."

"You don't have to leave."

"I do. We're flying to, um, gosh, I'm losing track." She looked to the headboard as though it had the answer. "Hartford, maybe. Leaving really early."

"You don't sound as if you enjoy this job. Quit."

"I can't. If I finish my contract and Trenton gets his nomination, I get a bonus." As she brought her chin back down, she adjusted the pearls so they weren't strangling her. "Before you think I'm all about the money, it's for Mom. She always wanted to go back to Paris. I promised her I'd sprinkle her ashes in the Seine."

"I'll take you," he offered smoothly.

"Please don't ruin this by suggesting I become your mistress," she admonished, both tempted and slighted. She'd thought they'd acted as equals here.

"I have companions, not mistresses," he corrected, pulling back and letting his hand fall on her stomach, but at a subliminal level, he'd pulled *way* back. "I don't buy women."

"Really. You don't support your lovers? Buy them clothes or jewelry? Take them on trips?" she asked skeptically.

"I meet their needs while they're with me, yes, and sometimes that extends to after we've stopped seeing each other. But it's not an exchange for sex."

"You're just that generous?"

"I try to be."

He sounded truthful, if stiffly reserved. Insulted?

"Well, I only have to get through the fall with this job and then I can look for something else. So I will," she said.

His lips twitched with dismay. "I don't like that answer," he informed her. "Quit now and look for something when it suits you."

Yes, she was a fool to think they were equals. Here was the rich tycoon who got what he wanted without regard for other people's wishes.

Proceeding delicately because she didn't want to ruin this fragile accord they'd managed to find, she said, "Roman, my mother put her fate in the hands of a powerful man, then birthed me into the same situation. It didn't work out well for either of us. I need my independence so I don't feel trapped or obligated."

"I'm not trying to trap you," he said with a scowl. "You could leave anytime."

"Then, I'll leave in the morning," she said gently.

He swore. "Walked into that one, didn't I?" He set his teeth. A muscle pulsed in his jaw. "I suppose I'll have to use other methods of persuasion." His gaze tracked back to hers and the heat in his eyes made her heart leap with panic.

"Don't!" She pressed her hands to his chest, holding him off as he started to tuck her beneath him.

He went motionless, only his head coming up slightly as he dragged his gaze from her nudity beneath him to the conflict that must be evident in her eyes.

"I'm not going to hurt you, Melodie," he said, brows coming together with concern.

"I think you might," she said, feeling her lips start to tremble. "You scare me, Roman. The way you make me feel. Please. If tonight is about making peace, please don't use my weakness against me."

He absorbed that in silence, only a small tick in his cheek letting her know he'd heard and was processing. Finally his mouth flattened in annoyance. "You're telling me I have to help you resist what we both want? *That* will hurt you, Melodie. I don't want to do that."

She didn't know much about computers, but she knew what circular logic was, and that was a big bunch of it right there. At the same time, her hands moved restlessly on him, smoothing his tight skin to his shoulders, pressing with involuntary invitation for him to lower onto her and kiss her.

They stole one brief kiss. Another. She could feel him hardening and opened her legs so he could settle properly between her thighs.

"I'm not going to deny you," he warned, smoothing her loose hair back from her face. "I'm going to give you everything you ask for. I'll stay just this side of barbaric as I ravish the hell out of you. If you can bring yourself to leave after that, I'll let you go."

Her heart trembled in her chest. Words stayed locked in her throat. All she could do was reach between them to guide him, telling him what she wanted. He teased her for a few moments, letting her feel his naked length against the growing ache in her loins, kissing her deeply until she was writhing with need beneath him. Then he covered himself and thrust, both of them catching ragged breaths as the agony of anticipation ceased and the perfection of joining commenced.

He was a man of his word; however, he dragged a pillow under her bottom so he could service her as thoroughly as possible, leaving her near weeping from the power of her release. Then he drew away, still hard, and proceeded to coax her down the road of sexual play all over again. He found all her erogenous zones and took his time stimulating her until she was ready for a firmer touch. A more insistent pull on her breast with his lips, a more erotic caress that he watched, soothing her when she tried to close her legs, claiming it was too immodest.

He gently dominated her then, rolling her so her stomach was on the pillow and covering her, but not taking her. He just stroked her with his body in a mimic of what they both wanted.

"Hurt?" he asked in a rasp. "I want everything in you, Melodie. Every last scream, but I won't take them. You have to give them to me."

She was sobbing, so aroused she was trembling. Shifting, coming up on her knees, she drew him to where she wanted him and clenched her fists in the sheets as he caressed her while he thrust. It was elemental and primitive, both of them stripped down to the very core. All her romantic notions of how men and women should come together dissolved in a flood of carnal hunger, decorum gone, both of them filling the room with erotic noises.

When they hit the peak, his fingers bit into her hips, locking them together as she cried, "Deeper, harder, yes, *yes*." He bucked and she gave up a long cry of gratified fulfillment.

CHAPTER EIGHT

ROMAN SWORE, SNAPPING Melodie from a doze.

"What's wrong?" she asked sleepily.

"Can't you hear it? Does he think he owns you?"

She lifted her head off his chest, where the steady thump of his heartbeat had lulled her. She heard the distant hum of her phone vibrating in the other room. Glancing at the clock, she said, "He's probably worried I'll miss the flight."

Roman's arm tightened on her.

She rolled onto him, growing addicted to the feel of his body against her own, loving the freedom to be like this: more than familiar or intimate. Close.

Nuzzling her nose into the fine hairs at his breastbone, she hid the dampness that rose behind her eyes as she drank in his scent, murmuring, "I have to leave soon. Not *should*," she clarified. "Have to."

"I heard you," he grumbled, massaging her scalp through the thick fall of her hair. "I still want you to stay."

"I'm glad," she said with a crooked smile, thinking of the way he'd thrown her out the first time. The remembrance didn't hurt as badly now. She had this incredible memory to replace it. "But I think in the long run we'd wind up in conflict. I do want love and marriage and kids, Roman. You were right about that."

His caress gentled to a light comb of his fingers through her hair. He didn't say anything. Didn't try to convince her he was a changed man, that they had a future. The silence caught at her tender heart, telling her she was making the right decision.

"But I could shower here," she suggested, lifting her head to offer a sultry look through tangled lashes, a smile pouted with invitation. "Rather than in my own room, alone."

"Deal."

Roman was jealous. He wasn't just annoyed on Melodie's behalf that her boss thought he had first call on her time. He was illogically threatened and nursing an uncomfortable state of rebuff as he walked away from her closed hotel room door and forced himself back to the elevator and his own room.

Emotions.

He eschewed them at every opportunity. Hope, happiness, pride. Those were all harbingers of a fall to come. That was what he'd learned through a very hard childhood. Better to focus on sensory pleasures and external goals that had a hope of being accomplished than seek some sort of inner fulfillment.

Melodie was right in saying they would run into conflict in the long run. She might act tough, but she was very sensitive, and he would wind up hurting her with his active attempts to feel nothing.

Which was exactly what he tried to do after walking her downstairs and returning to his empty suite. He was exhausted from lack of sleep, muscles aching from their night of marathon lovemaking, but he wasn't interested in crawling back into their wrecked bed. It looked too cold and empty. Unwelcoming.

Finding his scotch from the night before, he sipped it. It wasn't yet six and he hadn't slept, so that meant it was still last night, right?

One night. Since when did he feel depressed about any

woman leaving, whether it was within hours of their coming together or months?

Forget her, he insisted, thumbing across the screen on his phone to check his emails. Just as quickly he swept that screen aside and flicked to Melodie's contact card. Her number was still there. It hadn't accidentally been erased. Checking was completely juvenile, but asking her for it had been even more adolescent. He didn't chase women. He wouldn't call her. He had just wanted to know if she was willing to give it to him.

He wished he'd taken another shot of her this morning, clean faced and wearing a hotel robe, ball gown slung over her arm as she'd slowly closed the hotel room door on him. Her expression had been soft with sensual memory, her smile sweet and wistful.

How the hell did he even know what wistful looked like?

It looked like wanting what you couldn't have, he supposed, which was something he understood all too well. His childhood had been nonstop wishing. As an adult, he'd learned to get what he wanted or stop wanting it, very seldom coming up against a situation such as this.

I do want love and marriage and kids, she'd said. He turned that over in his mind, thinking how determined he'd been to find her in Virginia and take care of any child they might have conceived. There hadn't been any hesitation in him on that score, but what would things look like now if she had been pregnant? Would they be married?

He supposed there were conditions under which he would seek a lifetime commitment, but those conditions weren't *love*. His chest started to feel tight just thinking about opening himself up to that depth of emotion.

Damn it! Why the hell couldn't she have simply forgotten her pearls again and given him an excuse to call?

She'd taken them off at one point, but had asked for his help after her shower to put them back on.

He wandered the suite, scanning for forgotten items, finding only the hotel toothbrush she'd left in a glass next to the sink. Leaning in the bathroom doorway, staring at himself wearing his tuxedo pants and the shirt he'd been too lazy to close all the way, eyes dark with sleeplessness, shoulders slumped in defeat, Roman faced the fact he wasn't going to forget her. Ever.

Which tightened the vice in his chest a few more notches.

You don't tell me what you're thinking. He heard female voices complain from the past. *You go through the motions, but I don't feel like you really care.*

He cared. Cautiously. When it came to Melodie, he cared quite a bit. She was too sweet a person to deserve the battering of the Gautier gauntlet. He wanted to protect her from them, and he didn't care for this new, overbearing boss of hers one bit, either. He should have given her his number, told her to call anytime. For any reason.

Not bothering to overthink it, he dialed her number to tell her exactly that.

A male voice answered.

"Sadler?" Roman guessed, even though it didn't sound like him.

"This is his aide. Who's calling?"

"I'm looking for Melodie. It's Roman Killian."

A muffled conversation, then a voice he recognized. "Killian," Sadler said. "Melodie is no longer with us."

The worst emotion, the one she seemed to bring out in him most and which weighed the heaviest—guilt—descended on him. "You fired her," he deduced instantly. "For spending the night with me."

"I need my employees to be accessible at all times," Sadler said.

"But you told her to be nice to me," Roman said with

false conciliation. The man was lucky the sounds of traffic and car doors were coming through behind him, or Roman would be hunting him down in this hotel right now.

"Sluts become a liability," Sadler said. "You know that."

Roman closed his eyes, fighting the fire of rage that roared alive in him. Too intense. It had the power to murder. "I think you fired her because she wasn't nice to *you*. You're going to be very sorry *you* were not nicer to *her*."

Roman ended the call and strode out of his room, straight to Melodie's.

She didn't answer his knock, so he took the stairs down to the registration desk, asking them to ring her room.

"She's checked out, sir."

He bit back cursing aloud, his fist so tight on the marble desktop he could have shattered the stone with a single pound. She was probably in a taxi heading to the airport and back to Virginia—

Wait. A woman sat in the lobby restaurant wearing a fitted business suit. She had her shiny brown-gold hair pulled into a clip at her nape. Coffee steamed next to the tablet she had propped before her.

She was going to splash that coffee into his face, he thought, but went straight over anyway.

Roman threw his disheveled form into the chair opposite her. He'd showered with her, still smelled faintly of hotel soap, but he hadn't bothered shaving and, Lord, he was sexy with that stubble and hair that had dried uncombed. His shirt was still a deep, open V down his chest, the sleeves rolled back to his elbows. He was every woman's walking fantasy.

And he wore the most thunderous expression.

"Really?" he demanded. "I got you fired again. Really."

"It's like a gift, isn't it?" she said, thinking she ought to be more furious, but the relief was too profound. "Trenton phoned you to tell you? God, that's just like him. He waited until I was down here, you know. So he could do it in front of everyone. He didn't expect me to call him a hypocrite. Nice and loud, too. They all do it. I guarantee you all the other aides were picking up women in the bar while I was working the ballroom with him last night, but just because I'm a woman, I'm a slut. Men are such pigs."

As Roman turned his face away, his expression falling into weary lines, she found herself feeling sorry for him.

"Present company excluded, of course," she said.

He shook his head as if he couldn't believe what had happened. "I didn't mean to do this."

"You didn't," she said wearily. She was the one who had stayed in the penthouse with him, putting her physical gratification above her job, but she didn't get a chance to say so. The waitress arrived with her breakfast special.

"I'll have one of those," Roman said.

"Take mine," Melodie replied, snagging the fruit cup off the plate and nodding for the waitress to put the rest in front of Roman. "But he needs his own coffee."

He nodded agreement to the waitress, then looked at the plate of eggs and hash browns before him as if he couldn't face it. "You're giving me your breakfast? After I got you fired?"

"I had a voucher, but this was all I really wanted." She gently stirred the fresh berries into the yogurt beneath.

"How are you this forgiving? Because I want to slash the guy's tires. I want to slash my own," he added with self-disgust.

She shrugged. "I guess because I'd do it again," she said, hearing the poignant rasp in her voice as she recalled their night together.

"Would you?" He lowered his cutlery as he pinned her with a green stare as brilliant as the heart of a flame.

"I meant…" Wow. This wasn't going to be easy. He only

had to look at her. Focusing on chasing a blueberry with the tip of her spoon, she said, "I mean that, given the chance, I wouldn't have made a different decision last night. But the decision I made this morning still stands, Roman."

"Why?" he challenged immediately. "You don't have a job to go back to."

"I'm aware," she said tersely, glancing at the tablet that had gone black, but had conjured a handful of weak prospects a few seconds ago. "Rent is covered for next month, at least," she muttered. "But everything else is going to be a challenge."

Paris was out of the question for the foreseeable future.

"Melodie, you have to let me help you."

She shook her head. "I'll manage. I'm just bummed about Paris. I feel as if I'm letting Mom down." When her mother had refused treatment, had declined in such slow pain, the promise of Paris had been the only thing Melodie had been able to offer as comfort.

He reached across to take her wrist, thumb caressing the back of her hand. "Let me take you."

"Roman…" She turned her hand so she was gripping his fingers. "I *can't*."

"You can. You just don't want to." He pulled his hand away, jaw thrust out belligerently. He took up his fork with an air of impatience.

She acknowledged he was right with a jerk of her shoulder, wondering how he'd managed to make her feel guilty.

They ate in silence, breaking it only to thank the waitress when she cleared their plates.

Melodie took her last swallow of coffee, but struggled to get it down without choking as she realized this really was it. The end.

"Will you do something for me?" he asked, not letting on what was going on behind his aloof expression.

"Will you come up and let me show you something in my room?"

"Etchings?" she guessed facetiously. "I really should get to the airport. I'll be flying standby, so…"

"Please." He stood and shouldered her travel bag.

"You can't just tell me what it is?" She followed him to the elevator where she studied his enigmatic expression the whole way to the top floor. "You're being very mysterious," she said when he slid his key card into the reader.

"I'm really not," he said with a disparaging smirk, leaving her bag just inside the door. Moving to the bedroom, he jerked his chin at the bed.

"What?" She stood beside him to look at the rumpled sheets and indented pillows.

"We're both exhausted." He turned his head to give her a somnolent look. "Let's not make any decisions right now. I'm not asking for sex. I just can't think when I'm this tired. I become very one track, and all I know is that I want you there." He pointed at the bed.

"You really aren't mysterious, are you?" she said, struck by a wave of emotion that maybe came from tiredness, but also from what sounded like an oddly revealing statement from him.

She *was* tired. Stupid Trenton had waited for her to check out before cutting her loose, so she couldn't go back to her room and her own bed. She'd already been dreading the wait at the airport, trying to stay awake to hear if she'd been given a flight… It all began to look too overwhelming to face when there was a comfortable bed right there and a man peeling his shirt from his powerful chest.

She opened the button on her jacket, glanced at him with a small scold.

He said, "Thank you," in a quiet voice that was strangely soothing. She removed her jacket, gave it a shake, then folded it and laid it over the back of a chair. The rest of her clothes went neatly folded onto the seat. She kept on her underpants, but shed her bra, never comfortable sleeping in one. Instead, she picked up his shirt from where he'd dropped it on the floor and slid her arms into it.

"Do you mind?"

"Not a bit."

Closing a couple of buttons, she rounded the bed as he got in the other side. He held up the covers and she slid in beside him, feeling his arms close around her very comfortingly. Their bare legs braided together, and his lips nuzzled her hairline before he stole the clip from her hair and tossed it off the side of the bed.

Feeling secure and warm, Melodie let out a deep sigh. Roman's arms grew heavier on her, and that was all she remembered.

She woke to feel his erection straining the front of his shorts and pressing into her stomach. He was still asleep, but she couldn't help tracing the shape of him, already feeling liquid heat pooling between her legs in anticipation.

With a long inhale, Roman rolled onto his back, eyes opening to catch her gaze. They flashed with surprise and immediate desire.

"Come here," he said in a sleep-rasped voice, lifting his hips to push his boxers down and off before drawing her to straddle his thighs.

She removed her underwear and leaned for the condom herself before straddling his hips and covering him.

His hand came to the back of her neck and urged her down for a kiss. They rocked in ever-deepening caresses, wriggling and adjusting until he was penetrating, making her moan with indulgence. For a long time they barely moved, just kissed and enjoyed the sensation of being joined. She sat up to throw off his shirt and he starfished his hands over her breasts, letting her lean into his grip as she searched for a rhythm that made them both happy. It was good, so good, and lasted for a deliciously long time.

He was the one who said, "I'm going to explode," and slid his hand to her hip, thumb dipping inward to circle and incite.

The sharp sensation made her buck and seek more, so she moved urgently, flying them to a swift and sudden culmination that ended with him rolling her beneath him and kissing her deeply while the aftershocks played out.

Then came the reckoning. She didn't know how to leave after that. It had been too good.

He rolled away to dispose of the condom and she asked, "What time is it?" It came off sounding as though she had a train to catch. Funny, he'd made it sound as though a solid sleep would help her think more clearly, but she was more conflicted than ever now.

"Two." He rolled back and caught her hand, bringing her fingertip to the gentle bite of his teeth. "Our body clocks are going to be a real mess when we get to France."

"Nice try." She smiled, admiring his confidence. "But I'm not quite ready to head to Paris yet. There are a lot of hoops to jump through when you want to transport ashes. I've been wading through bureaucracy for months."

"I'll make a call," he said, weaving their fingers together.

"To whom?" she demanded. "It's not easy, you know."

He dismissed that with a snort. "I'm an approved government supplier in both America and France. I have contacts."

"I wouldn't say no to a call," she conceded. "Anything that could streamline that side of things would be a huge favor, but, Roman—"

"Listen," he said in a grave tone. "I didn't have the chance to do anything for my mother when she died. If there was a service, I wasn't invited. I want to do this."

She blinked, surprised. "Why not? What happened?"

He fell onto his back, untangled their fingers to tuck his fist beneath the pillow under his head. For a moment she thought he wasn't going to answer. She couldn't read a thing on his face and, as the silence lengthened, she felt as though she'd transgressed. He was spurning her, and it left her feeling bereft.

"If you don't want to talk about it—"

"I don't," he said. "But I should. If I want you to stay, you have to know who I am. I was nine when she died. I had already been in foster care for a few years. She…" His face worked, fighting for control. "She had resorted to prostitution to feed me. Ironically, that's why she lost me. She was just doing it until I was in school. I remember her telling me everything would be better once I started school and she got a real job, not that I really understood what she was doing. That came later, but…"

Shock closed cold fingers around Melodie's heart.

"Then I was taken from her, so she did get a job, except it was a terrible one in a sweatshop. There was a fire. I realize there wouldn't have been a body for me to see, but they didn't even tell me when it happened. It took weeks. I kept asking if I could call and there would be all these muttered conversations, and finally they told me she was in heaven. It took years to find out heaven is actually Hart Island, where the poor and homeless are buried in mass, unmarked graves. There hadn't been any money for a service, so there wasn't one."

"Oh, Roman, I'm so sorry." She set a comforting hand on his chest.

He caught it. For a moment she thought he was going to reject her touch, but after a few seconds, his hand flexed on hers and he swallowed. "Every time I talked to her, I asked her when she was going to come get me." His voice had thickened. "She took that stupid job for me."

She opened her mouth, but only a burn of anguish came in, searing her lungs. Settling over him, she pressed her face into his neck and offered the only comfort she could.

Roman stiffened as Melodie blanketed him in compassion. It was almost cloying, making his old grief too fresh and unbearable. He wanted to push her away, push all of it away, but after a second her scent penetrated to the most primitive part of his brain. Things he associated with her, such as softness and forgiveness and pleasure, pulled him back from falling into the dark emotions that talking about his mother had opened up.

Jerkily he closed his arm around Melodie's slender frame, sealing her silken nudity against his own bare skin.

They lay like that a long time. It was strange. He wanted to roll into her and forget all of it with the pursuit of physical gratification, but he wanted to stay like this, too. Still and calm, in quiet harmony.

Maybe they dozed, because the buzz of his phone on vibrate made Roman jerk in surprise. Since he'd pretty much been off the grid for nearly twenty-four hours, he sat up to find his pants and looked at the screen. Melodie's number flashed back at him.

"Looks like you're calling me," he told her, answering with "Sadler?"

"His aide again, Mr. Killian. We're wondering, is Melodie with you?"

"She is." He glanced at her.

She sighed and gathered the sheet across her breasts as she sat up and held out a resigned hand.

Roman kept the phone.

"May I speak to her?" the aide asked in a tone of tested patience.

"No," Roman said. "Lose this number. I don't want to hear from you again."

"Wait! Ask her to call us. We're looking for a file and can't find—"

"No," Roman repeated firmly. "Remind Sadler that I told him he'd regret not being nicer to her. Let him know that I'll be making some calls to his biggest corporate sponsors, too. Melodie can give me that list, I'm sure."

"We're prepared to reinstate her," the aide rushed to say.

"I'm not going to tell her you said that. And if you even think about making her life difficult because of this, you're going to find out exactly how vindictive I can be. Am I making myself clear?"

After a beat of silence, the aide said tightly, "Let me pass this over to Trenton."

"Don't bother." Roman ended with a cheerful yet filthy suggestion for the bunch of them and stabbed a button to end the call.

Melodie tucked her chin, admonishing him, "I heard them offer me my job back."

"And you didn't speak up."

She sighed, knees coming up so she could hug them, then set her chin on them. "Do you really want to help me with Mom? Like, would it help you?"

He dropped his gaze from the earnest softness in hers. He was still pulsing with the sort of discontent that came from smashing your own thumb with a hammer, sorry that he'd told her something so personal. It was the kind of intimate detail he never, ever gave up about himself. Especially if it was going to make someone look at him like that.

So did he expect that going through a memorial of some kind with her mother would *help* him? No. It would stir up this turmoil inside him that he'd spent years sublimating. Was he willing to put himself through it to keep Melodie with him?

Bizarrely, the answer was yes.

"Let me make that call," he said.

CHAPTER NINE

THREE DAYS LATER Roman flew Melodie by private jet to Paris. They discovered that rivers and streams were off-limits for scattering ashes, but found a special remembrance garden where they were able to spend a reflective hour settling Patience into the state of peace that had eluded her in her living years.

"Thank you," Melodie said, reaching across the back of the limo to take Roman's hand as they left the gated cemetery. She was hollowed out, eyelids stinging and swollen from crying, throat still scratchy, but she felt at ease for the first time in years. Maybe since the first time she had fully realized what sort of tortured existence her mother had led. "I couldn't rest until I'd given her that. Nothing can hurt her now. This means a lot to me. Thank you."

"You're welcome." His distant, faintly wooden response might have struck her as disinterested if she hadn't seen him struggle several times during the small ceremony she'd arranged. She remembered him calling himself emotionally inaccessible, and he certainly kept his cards close to his chest, but he wasn't indifferent. As he'd cradled her against him when they'd been left alone to say their good-byes, she suspected he'd offered a much-delayed farewell to his own mother.

Not that she would intrude to ask.

Instead, she twisted her head on the seat to look at him. "When you told me you try to meet the needs of your companions, did you ever see yourself doing something like this?"

That caught him by surprise, making him laugh. "No," he pronounced drily, faint grin lingering.

"Well, I appreciate your making an exception," she teased, leaning across to kiss his cheek.

He cupped the back of her head, keeping her close for a few short, sweet kisses on her lips.

"Where are we going now?" she drew back to ask. They'd flown overnight, arriving about six in the morning Virginia time, and had come straight to the cemetery for a midday ceremony. She wasn't sure if she was tired or hungry or what.

"What do you want to do?" he asked easily.

"I'm not sure." The sky had been low when they'd landed, but was brightening by the minute, and she kept seeing trees in blossom against rain-washed stone, tulips and cafés and smiling couples. "Could we walk around the city a bit?"

"Of course." He had a word with the driver and they pulled over a moment later.

For the next two hours they wandered aimlessly past flower stalls and into shops for pastries. When she paused to examine the price tag on a newsboy cap in olive green with a cute floral band wrapped into a smart little buckle, he plopped it on her head and held out his credit card to the proprietress.

"I was only thinking about it," she said, adjusting it in the mirror after the tag had been removed.

"It suits you."

"Well, thank you," she said cautiously. Accepting a gift from him was a slippery slope. She was already indebted to him for the flight, and he hadn't been satisfied with making this a weekend trip, stating he had business to take care of later in the week.

Since they were staying at his apartment and he wasn't footing the bill on a hotel, she had acquiesced. She fully intended to cook for him while they were here, but when she mentioned picking up a few groceries, he said, "I made reservations. For an early sitting since I knew we'd be tired. I've been steering us toward the club. It's only another block over. We should change, though. I was going to leave you next door and walk across to the men's shop."

"Next door" was a boutique where the saleswomen greeted "Monsieur Killian" by name. One even pressed her cheek to his and said something warm in French that made Melodie's toes curl in dismay. When he mentioned where they were going, the women began pulling out black cocktail dresses that didn't have price tags *at all*.

"Roman," Melodie started to protest.

"Take your time. I'll come back when I'm finished and they'll pour me a drink while I wait over there." He nodded to a small but luxurious lounge area. "I know the drill."

"Because you've done this before?" she guessed.

He heard the edge in her tone. His own cooled. "I have. Although never to this specific jazz club. They have a female blues singer there. You said your mother used to listen to French blues. I thought you'd enjoy it."

Which sounded very thoughtful of him, but...

"I'd like to take you on a proper date, Melodie," he added. "We haven't had one yet."

Yes, they had, but he didn't stick around to hear her argue that dinner and a movie in Virginia was a perfectly acceptable date. Another night, she had cooked for him and he'd run out for a bottle of wine, bringing back flowers, as well.

"Mademoiselle?" the boutique owner prompted.

In the end, after their afternoon of walking, Melodie found herself grateful for a reason to sit down and sip a fortifying glass of champagne and freshly squeezed orange juice while dresses were brought to her for consideration. Crackers appeared with foie gras and caviar, salty and delicious.

As for the dresses, the sleek, modern designs with cutouts and daring necklines were beautiful, but Melodie's eye kept tracking back to something a bit more modest with a hint of flounce. The bodice was silk organza, fitted in the front and disappearing behind her shoulders into a backless pair of straps. The skirt was short and narrow, but had a fuller sheer overlay that added femininity and swung sassily. Beaded detailing at the waist gave the dress more of a figure-eight figure than her stalk-like build usually had.

The saleswomen made several admiring remarks about her *jambes* after she tried it on with a pair of deceptively simple black high heels with detailing down the tall, wickedly sharp heel. One suggested if she lost six or eight kilos, she could find work in Paris as a model.

"Kilos," Melodie repeated. "Those are bigger than pounds, right?" *Fifteen pounds? Really?*

They weren't being catty, though. They were actually very nice. Maybe Roman paid them to be, but Melodie still felt pampered and relaxed by the time she had her hair styled to cloud around her face and her eyes smokily made up so the blue of her irises popped.

Then a funny attack of nerves hit her as she walked out to greet Roman. Even as a teenager living off her generous allowance, she had never taken this much care with her appearance. Anton had always made her believe it was futile to try. She'd resigned herself to never affecting boys and had rarely wanted so badly to impress a man.

Roman was looking at his phone, a drink on the side table next to him, his arm stretched out to rest along the back of the sofa. His new white shirt fit him just this side of bursting its seams, hugging his muscles and pulling across his chest. The collar was turned up and his hair had been given a professional ruffle. He hadn't shaved since just before they landed and the shadow on his cheeks and jaw gave him a rakish air.

He sat with his ankle crooked up to rest on his knee, straining the fabric of his black pants, which were tailored to showcase his toned thighs. Argyle socks peeked between the cuff of his pants and his shiny shoes.

He was so casually hot she had to stop to catch her breath.

Then he looked up and stole her breath all over again.

Only his eyes moved as they leisurely traveled from her hair in its big, loose curls, to the glossy pink lips she tried not to ruin by pressing them together instead of licking them, to the ever-present pearls against her collarbone. Her shoulders twitched and her breasts prickled as she felt his gaze caress her there, then her stomach sucked in and her intimate muscles clenched when he stroked her bare legs with his gaze.

"Turn around," he commanded huskily.

Swallowing, she suppressed the feminist in her that scolded her for letting herself be objectified, arguing that this was different. This was…

She turned her back, her entire body coming alive under the awareness that she had his complete attention. When she turned again to see him, he was rising in an easy flex of his strong frame. He came toward her, and she reminded herself, *Breathe, idiot, breathe.*

"You're beautiful," he murmured, lips grazing her brow as she dipped her chin self-consciously. His hands settled on her bare arms in a light, tantalizing caress while the starchy smell of new clothes came off him along with a fresh sample of cologne and his own masculine notes.

"I feel beautiful," she said. It wasn't just the dress and the makeup. It was the way he reacted to her every min-

ute of every day. He complimented her whether she was
coiffed and made-up or disheveled and wearing a house-
coat. Today was simply the day she embraced his words as
true. "I do," she said sincerely. "Now. Thank you."

"How could you ever doubt it?" he scoffed lightly.

She debated, not wanting to spoil the moment, but she
wanted him to understand how much confidence he gave
her.

"You already know my upbringing wasn't the best.
Anton hated that Dad had remarried and it didn't matter
that I was his half sister. No matter what I wore or said,
he put me down. It's taken a long time to get past it. But
since I have so much more respect for your opinion than
his," she said ruefully, "I *must* be beautiful."

His expression had grown sober as he'd listened, then
he gently caressed her cheek. "There will be a correction,
Melodie. Rest assured I'm taking note, and the extent of
their crimes will not go unpunished."

"Don't— I didn't say that so you'd stoop to their level."

"I know. And I won't. But I'm not as forgiving as you
are. Mark my words, when the time is right they'll receive
their reckoning. But let's not spoil our evening thinking
about them." He tugged her into his big frame.

Her hands went to his waist and splayed, taking in heat
and firm, taut man. She could get used to leaning on him.
Easily. Far too easily.

"Ready to go?" he asked, breath faintly scented with
scotch.

"I don't know how far I can walk in these shoes," she
said, lifting a foot so he could see the wicked spike.

"The car's outside."

The boutique owner carried out Melodie's things in a
bag and handed them to the chauffeur while Roman helped
her into the backseat.

Moments later he helped her out again and they entered

a nightclub lit only by candles and subtly recessed indigo bulbs. Glowing white tablecloths draped tiny tables surrounded by comfortable chairs. The glassware sparkled and the servers wore tuxedos. The place was already full, but they were shown to a reserved table in an elevated alcove that allowed them some privacy yet offered a perfect view of the stage.

The meal was served in a series of courses between sets, the food excellent, while the chanteuse created a warmly nostalgic mood that allowed Melodie to envision her mother as a young model in Paris, briefly happy.

Roman leaned his arm on the back of her chair and played with her hair. She set her hand on his thigh and wondered if this was a dream. They even danced, although it was more a prelude to what would come later. Like every other couple, they plastered themselves to each other and swayed lazily, using the music as an excuse to arouse each other.

Weakly tilting her head back so she could see him, she didn't have to say a word.

"I'm ready, too," he said hungrily, and tightened his arms on her so she could feel how hard he was. "I'll call for the car."

She was past the point of trying to understand it. Between New York and Virginia, they'd been making love every time they found a shred of privacy. She was shocked by how constant their desire was, but she'd stopped fighting it. She was only grateful the distance to his apartment was short.

Expecting a high-rise, she was surprised when the car halted outside an art gallery. A bright glow came through the windows and a chic crowd mingled inside.

"Are we going in?" she asked as they stepped onto the sidewalk.

"My flat is upstairs." He walked her to a steel door next to the gallery entrance, slid open a panel and peeked inside.

The door cracked open. Inside was a small closet for coats and shoes, then a flight of stairs to an open-plan bachelor apartment. No sound from the crowd below penetrated, and the lighting was all indirect and moody.

Melodie took in exposed brickwork, high ceilings and elegant white furniture in a lounge containing ferns and colorful throws. A butcher-block island with copper cookware suspended above it separated the kitchen and its stainless-steel appliances from the rest of the apartment. Floating stairs led to a bedroom in a loft. The bedding looked sumptuous with its rich colors and tasseled pillows. Beneath the loft was a cozy library with bookshelves and a pretty antique desk that was probably strong enough to hold a laptop, but was more for looks than serviceability.

"This is not your apartment," she said decidedly.

"Why do you say that? My iris is the one that opens the door. And the housekeeper's," he allowed. "She comes in once a week. Which reminds me. Open."

He came toward her with his phone, holding it before one of her eyes, which widened in stern outrage.

"This is your love nest," she accused as he clicked.

He didn't respond to that immediately, taking his time tapping the screen before tucking his phone in his shirt pocket. "You saw how I slid open the reader. It's painless. No flash or anything. Just look into it and the door will open."

She folded her arms. "You're not going to admit you bring women here?"

"I have an office here in Paris," he said. "With accommodations attached. Very utilitarian. If I'm here strictly for work, I usually stay there."

"But if you have a companion, you tuck her up here."

"If it bothers you that you're not the only woman who

has stayed with me here, we can get a hotel." He showed no emotion, completely matter-of-fact about it.

"It bothers me that you're maneuvering me into being your *companion*," she said. "This is nice," she hurried to add, sweeping her hands to indicate the gorgeous outfit she wore and the beautiful flat. "But I can't let you take over, Roman. I can't—"

"Is that what it is? Melodie," he cut in with gentle firmness. He came forward to take her flinging hand in both of his. "The first day we met you said there was only one way to get to know a person, and that was by spending time with them. I want to spend time with you."

"I'd like to get to know you better, too, but—"

"I can't sit in Virginia waiting for you to find a job that will keep you out all day. Listen, I understand not wanting to rely on people. I'm a foster kid. I was always a guest, always a burden. I hated that feeling. But now I'm someone who can pay and pay back. I want you to let me."

He was taking all her arguments, defusing them and setting them aside like empty milk bottles.

"It seems wrong," she mumbled weakly.

"You're not taking advantage of me. This is my decision. Do you really want to go back to Virginia?" he asked, playing dirty by drawing her against him so she was surrounded by all things Roman: his warm strength and the animal scent that went straight into her brain and shorted it out. A streaking sensation of kindled desire followed the brush of his lips from her temple down her cheek to her nape.

"No," she allowed, throwing back her head so he could nibble the sensitive skin in a way that softened her knees. "But you're not playing fair," she complained.

"And if you stay I will play unfair to you as often as you want me to," he promised, biting lightly into her earlobe. "Would you like that?"

A shiver of acute need chased through her.

"Yes," she admitted.

"Here? Or somewhere else?"

She almost hated him in that moment, wishing she had the strength to insist on going somewhere that he hadn't taken other women when he obviously had the capacity to hold off and she didn't.

"Here," she moaned weakly, chasing his mouth with her own.

"Good," he growled. "Because I can't wait."

They didn't even make it up the stairs, christening his Turkish rug instead.

CHAPTER TEN

THE WEEK IN Paris passed in a pleasant blur of lovemaking and walking tours of the old part of the city. And, when Roman had time to join her, they window-shopped and he bought her whatever she showed the least bit of interest in. He was too generous, buying her a new outfit for every dinner, cocktail party or gala cruise on the Seine. If he didn't buy her something while they were out, he brought her flowers or, this morning, a fancy new mobile phone.

"Roman, I can't."

She was starting to feel as though all the spoiling was his way of compensating for the fact he didn't offer much of himself. He was the most attentive lover she could ask for, but when it came to anything really personal, he was very adept at turning the conversation in another direction.

"You're doing me a favor. It's a prototype. It needs to be tested." He showed her how to log feedback for anything that didn't work to her satisfaction. "If they don't notify you of an update that fixes it within twenty-four hours, tell me. I'll follow up. Look, it has a GPS so I can track you down wherever you are and join you."

"Or you could call me and ask," she supplied with a chipper smile. "What about a cover? I don't want to break it."

"It's unbreakable and waterproof. If it's not, my suppliers will answer for it." He went on with nerdy enthusiasm about its space-age alloys and special screen, the airtight design and its ability to be compressed into a diamond if dropped under a steamroller. "If you lose it, we can track it to within a meter, but try not to lose it. I might misplace my temper if you do. And if you sell it, do not settle for less than a quarter of a million euros or I will be highly insulted."

"Roman!" she cried. "I can't walk around with a phone worth that kind of money! And who is likely to buy a phone that costs that much?" she asked with sudden puzzlement. "Have you thought this through?"

"Your half brother would easily pay that much for this phone," he stated flatly, then quirked a brow as he added pithily, "When it goes to market it will retail for a few hundred dollars, competing with the rest of the smart-phones. At the moment, however, the technology is fresh and incredibly secure to use. Far better than anything else currently available. My competitors would be extremely interested in breaking it down before it's released."

"And you're trusting me with it?" she asked with awe, hugging the hard shape to her breast. She swallowed back a rush of emotion, moved to tears. "I mean, the way we met…"

"I trust you, Melodie," he said, sounding sincere.

She melted inside. Of all the gifts he could have given her, his trust was the most touching. It cracked the last of her resistance against letting him support her. She wanted rather desperately to stay with him and see where this re-lationship could go.

That afternoon she used the credit card he'd given her for the first time—in a lingerie shop. She figured the pur-chase was really for him, and he was highly appreciative when she modeled it for him later.

And since they were getting along so beautifully, when she sprawled atop him, her lacy underthings askew, and he said, "I have to be in Germany on Tuesday," she lifted her head and said, "Do you mind if I charge a suitcase to the card? You've bought me too many outfits. They won't all fit in mine."

"I told you what your limit was. Charge anything you like to it." He tucked a wisp of her hair behind her ear. "But leave a few things here for when we come back."

"When will that be?" she asked with surprise.

"I don't know. Probably not until after the summer. I have some meetings in Italy next month and I thought we could spend some time on my yacht after that, but eventually we'll come back here."

After the summer. The words sent a funny, exciting sensation into the pit of her belly. Maybe they did have a future.

Roman was in a perfect place. Of all the women he'd dated over the years, few had been such a good match for him on every level as Melodie. Definitely the sex was better than any man had a right to, sometimes playful, sometimes erotic, always intensely satisfying. Professionally, he couldn't ask for a better partner by his side. She not only sparkled like a sapphire, lighting up a room, but she knew how to strike exactly the right balance of warmth with boundaries. Aside from the sparest of details such as where they might have eaten dinner or which part of a city they were staying in, she shared nothing of their private life with anyone.

When they were alone she was equally capable of being a charming, amusing companion, yet always respected his retreat after questions such as, "Do you know anything about your father?" and "What were the foster homes like? Were you safe there?"

No, he didn't know anything about his father. No, he hadn't always been safe. There'd been good ones and bad ones, the most important thing being that they had been impermanent. Buying the house in France, along with being a status symbol, was also his way of creating a proper home for himself. A place he could and always would return to. Why France? He liked the climate.

He didn't know why he couldn't simply say that to her. Because he had long ago programmed himself to keep such things private, he supposed.

And she seemed okay with the status quo, so he didn't see any need to change.

Until she had an issue with her phone and he wound up being called in to help troubleshoot. That was when he learned Melodie not only had been looking for work in Virginia, but also had even looked up one-way flight details for a week from now.

The blood seemed to drain out from his toes, leaving him staring at a screen that didn't make sense while his agile mind froze, needing a reboot. For a few long minutes he wasn't even sure he was breathing. All he could think was *She can't leave*.

Despite his attempts to keep his feelings for her light, he was struck by how much she was coming to mean to him. It made his joints grate like sandpaper as he rose and went to find her where she was reading her tablet next to the pool off his penthouse here in Rome.

He set down her phone on the table beside her, lowered himself onto the side of the lounger alongside hers and confronted reality in the way he'd learned to do. "You're thinking of leaving?"

Surprise flashed in her blue gaze before she glanced at her phone and said, "You looked at my browsing history?"

"For the search-engine problems you were having. I wasn't trying to spy." He betrayed no hint of defensiveness. All his feelings were firmly buried in the sealed vault behind the barred door, in the bottom of the abandoned building that was his mortal coil. "The job board came up."

She tucked her chin downward, half sheepish, half admonishing. "I'm not used to being idle, Roman. It's making me a little crazy, doing nothing. I enjoyed Berlin and obviously Rome has an amazing history..." She frowned at the view of the Coliseum amid the rest of the red-tile rooftops across the city. "But it's not really as if I'm on vacation. Not with you anyway. You're working. I thought I might be able to find something that I could do remotely."

Okay. He could see that, but "Why the flight, then?"

"Oh, that was for a friend. She's been traveling around Europe and thought she might be able to join us here for a few days if she could change her flight home."

The relief was so great in him he almost slumped forward, but he was highly experienced at not betraying his reactions. He only nodded. "You're not planning on leaving, then."

"No." She searched his gaze and, he was quite sure, found little of his thoughts. "Not unless you want me to," she added hesitantly.

"I don't." He could see the uncertainty in her, the need for reassurance. He felt a discord in himself, too, as if they'd had a conflict and even though it had been easily ironed out, something more was needed. Still, he only rose and said, "How do you feel about organizing the launch party for the phone? Marketing is already working on the timeline, but planning the event would be very much within your forte. Would you like that?"

"If you would like me to do it, then, sure."

"I'll inform them now." He walked away, knowing he should have taken more steps to close the gap between them, but it had taken everything in him to face the possible dissolution of their arrangement. The spring of emotion at their staying together was too raw and concentrated to work through anywhere but in complete solitude.

Melodie nursed a let-down feeling until that night when she and Roman went to bed, practically acting like an old married couple in the way they brushed teeth and undressed, crawled in under the covers and snuggled close for a kiss good-night.

Their good-night kisses almost always turned into lovemaking, but tonight it turned into something that went beyond it. Roman was so hard, so urgent, he pressed into her almost before she was ready, making her flinch a little at the sting.

He groaned an apology and seemed to gather his control at that point, ensuring her pleasure again and again while he possessed her, imprinting her with his scent and touch and branding kisses to the point where she nearly wept with joy and fulfillment.

Later, in the sultry dark, pinned against him by arms that had closed tightly around her, she rubbed her cheek against his chest.

"I wish you would tell me what you're thinking and feeling," she murmured.

A long pause, then: "I know."

Part of her suspected he *had* told her exactly what was going on inside him, but what if she was interpreting things wrong?

Two days later Roman and Melodie moved onto his yacht, sailing toward Sardinia with the intention of visiting both that island and Corsica before making their way to his home near Cannes. At least now he was working from his office on board, inviting her to interrupt him at any time. They were closer physically if not emotionally.

She told herself they just needed time. If she had any

doubts about him, she just had to look at his actions rather than wait for words. Her life really couldn't get much better than it currently was.

"Is there any way to improve the camera features on the phone?" she asked him one evening over dinner, feeling like a spoiled brat since, really, the camera was already quite good. But she'd resurrected a hobby she'd enjoyed as a teenager and handed over her phone so he could see the shots she'd taken thus far. "It's better than any other phone out there, I know. And part of me enjoys the challenge of getting what I want despite its limitations, but there are some things I'd like to try that just aren't here— What's wrong?"

"Nothing. These shots are very good. I tend to think of you being a natural in front of the camera. I didn't realize you had such talent behind one."

"I don't. It's just something to keep me busy," she dismissed.

The next day a high-end digital camera showed up with a dozen lenses and other pieces of equipment.

Melodie didn't even bother scolding him. She was too delighted.

She was happy. Happier than she'd ever been, so she ignored how tenuous things felt, not wanting to cause ripples.

Which was why the call from her father a few days later nearly had her dropping her brand-new camera onto the deck. When her phone rang she was so distracted with trying to work out one of the high-tech menu options, she picked up the call very absently, expecting Roman was being too lazy to come and find her from his office.

"Charmaine," her father said, and she managed to catch the camera with her thighs and drop herself into a cushioned chair. Her stomach curdled. She hated that name. It was his mother's name, and she'd been a horrible woman, bullying Melodie's mother in a hundred ways, not the least of which being her insistence of being the namesake of her granddaughter.

"What—?" she asked faintly, unable to compute. "How did you get this number?"

"That doesn't matter. The fact you have a new lover is the important piece here."

Her fingers were going numb, her mind racing. "It's none of your business."

"Oh, I assure you it's very much our business. Something we're going to turn to our advantage."

"How?" she choked. "By stealing from him again? There is nothing you can do to make me do *anything* for you." Hysteria edged into her tone. "You have nothing to offer me. Nothing to hold over me." A distant memory came to her of Roman using a certain phrase. "Lose this number," she spat. "I don't ever want to hear from you again." She drew her arm back, ready to throw her beloved phone into the sea.

A hand caught hers from behind, nearly making her jump out of her skin.

Roman.

Oh, God.

She knew instantly by his grim expression that even if he hadn't heard everything that had been said, he knew who she was talking to. He would believe she'd betrayed him and this would all be over, everything they had—

He pried the phone from her vice-like grip and ended the call, then moved so he stood facing her.

"I didn't call him," she stammered out quickly, beginning to shake. "I don't even know how he got the number." Her vision blurred as she grew convinced he was about to reject her. It was like seeing the car coming, yet having her feet stuck in cement. "I'm sorry," she started to babble. "I didn't know what to do—"

"Melodie," he said firmly. "You did the right thing." He

set aside her phone and squatted in front of her, stilling her trembling hands as she tried to keep the camera in her lap. "Aside from the part where you nearly gave my prototype a burial at sea. Although it might have been a fun exercise using the signal to retrieve it."

"Don't make jokes," she said, fighting tears, clinging to his hands with cold fingers. "Maybe it was my neighbor, the one getting my mail and watering my plants," she sniffed, brain starting to work as she realized Roman wasn't going to throw her overboard. She swiped at the wetness tracking to the corner of her mouth. "She doesn't know anything about my relationship with him. If he got hold of her, she probably would have thought it was okay to give him my number. Roman, I'm so sorry. I don't want him badgering us, making trouble—"

"He won't," he assured her, sounding so confident, the tears simply wouldn't stay put behind her lashes.

She laughed bitterly. "I don't think of you as a naive man, but surely you realize that he'll do awful things now, try to get between us. Why didn't I see this coming?"

"Melodie," he chided, cupping the side of her face and brushing a thumb beneath her overflowing eye. "I'll have the number changed. You won't hear from him again. Now please stop crying. I don't like seeing you upset by him."

"He'll keep trying!" she insisted.

"Let him try. I won't let him near you. Believe me." So commanding.

"How could you possibly stop him?" she asked, accosted by the kind of hopelessness she'd thought she'd managed to escape for good, that feeling that a dark lord could leap out of the shadows to rake her through the coals of hell at any moment. "I don't know why I didn't see that being with you, of all people, would make him—" She would have to break up with him if she expected to find any sort of peace.

Roman scowled, silently regarding her for a long, frustrated minute, before his brows lifted and a smile ghosted across his lips. "I'll call our new friend, Nic Marcussen."

"What for? No. Please don't! He already thinks I'm an idiot!" Day two with her new camera, she'd trained her lens on the dolphins dancing against the media mogul's bow, completely unaware she was also snapping shots of his family. Apparently he was extremely protective of his children and had insisted on boarding Roman's yacht ten minutes later, stealing Melodie's memory card and returning it minus several of her best shots.

Roman had not been pleased, but more because he could see how upset Melodie was, not because she'd got him off on the wrong foot with one of the world's most powerful men. They'd actually wound up having drinks later when they'd both anchored in the same cove. Nic's wife was a peach, but Melodie still felt as if she'd grossly invaded their privacy. It had been a good lesson in requesting permission before clicking the shutter.

"He never paid you for the shots he appropriated."

"I didn't want him to!" When Nic had offered to pay her the scale rate for news photos, she'd been horrified, wanting to erase the whole mortifying experience. "It was too much anyway. I'm just an amateur."

Roman gave her a patronizing look. "Your amateur shots are better than many professionals', and you know it. And if you'd accepted his payment, you would be a professional yourself. Come with me."

She dragged her feet as she followed him into his office and watched as he called Nic on his tablet. "Melodie needs a favor," Roman said. "Are you aware that her father is Garner Gautier? Have you heard of him?"

"On occasion," Nic said with reserve.

"Sounds as though you know what kind of man he is.

Melodie is thinking of writing a memoir about her child-hood. Quite a tell-all."

"No, I'm not!" she cried, shaking her head vehemently.

"You're offering me exclusive rights to this memoir?" Nic asked.

Both men ignored her protests, talking over her.

"That's right," Roman continued.

"Roman, no!" Melodie insisted. "I don't want to profit from my family's dirty laundry. My mother's memory doesn't need that kind of smearing and neither do I. *No.*"

"I could give Gautier a call, ask him if he'd like to con-tribute his side of things?" Nic suggested.

"You see where I'm going with this. I knew this was the right call to make."

Melodie didn't. "Both of you, stop. I really don't want all that to come out. There would be paparazzi, a complete media circus…"

Roman clasped a reassuring hand on her arm. "It's never going to come out, Melodie."

"Gautier is going to pay back your advance to me so I will kill the book before it's written," Nic explained. "And that figure would be…?"

"Not a penny less than three million. Five would be better," Roman said.

"That's blackmail," Melodie gasped, pulling from his grip to cross her arms.

"It's a message," Roman insisted. "He doesn't have to pay, but he'll understand the potential consequences if he comes near you again. If he does pay, well, think of all the programs that money could beef up at your mother's clinic."

"It's still bribery," she stated, but she was warming to this outlandish idea.

"And since Nic taking your photos was larceny…"

"By all means, let me redeem myself," Nic said drily.

And that was that. They left it with Nic, and Melodie spent the afternoon quietly reeling. Later that night, when she felt an urgent wave of attraction, as though she couldn't get enough of Roman, he accommodated her very tenderly, overpowering her to slow her down, whispering, "It's okay, Melodie. It's okay."

She wasn't so sure. For a short while she'd been terrified she would lose him. It had been the most painfully lonely vision of her future she could imagine.

But she didn't lose him. One week on the Med turned into two, then three. Roman worked every day and Melodie filled her time with photography, joining amateur forums online for tips and critiques, thinking of starting a blog just to have a reason to share her best shots.

It was an incredibly easy existence after so many years of hardship. She didn't know how to handle it and it bothered her sometimes, made her think she wasn't trying hard enough or wasn't paying her dues. Rather than relaxing into confidence that they were a solid couple, she grew more and more anxious that something would tear them apart.

Maybe if he showed more emotion, she found herself thinking as she stood at the rail, photographing their approach to his beachside home. But despite weeks of close proximity, she really didn't know Roman much better than she had the first time she'd arrived at this elegant home.

"I just told Ingrid you're my date for her wedding tomorrow," he said as he joined her.

Talk about leaving things to the last minute. Melodie lowered the camera. "What did she say?"

He shrugged negligently, not surprising her a bit when that was the sum total of his reply.

She sighed and lifted the camera again. "I suppose I should be grateful you didn't just appear with me by your side without any explanation at all," she groused.

"Our being together wasn't any of her business until now."

"Is that really why you waited this long to say anything?" she asked.

"What do you mean?"

She pretended to change the menu options on the back of the camera, but really just clicked through the settings. "I can't help thinking you weren't sure if we'd still be together, so you skipped mentioning it until you knew for sure that we would be."

"And now you're picking a fight to put that in jeopardy?"

"No," she grumbled.

"I'm a private man, Melodie. You know that."

This time when she sighed, it was much heavier, laden with impatience. "I am aware, yes. I'd love to know why talking is so hard for you, but wouldn't dare ask."

Silence.

Misgivings rolled in like fog, making her feel chilled, as if her breaths were wet and thick.

"I'm sorry," she said, sincere, but even she could hear the tone she was taking. Frustration flattened the apology. "I really don't want to pick a fight. I was just feeling…" *Insecure.* She didn't want to admit it.

"You're hardly the first woman to become annoyed with me," he allowed.

"Oh, good. Compare me to the rest of your *companions*. That'll smooth things over. What's that white thing out there?" she asked, swiftly changing topics to avoid a bigger fight. "Is that the water doing that? Churning up or something?"

"It's a rip current," he said testily, taking a step toward the rail. He glanced from the water to the interior of the yacht, as if he couldn't decide whether he wanted to stick around and work out the niggle between them or escape it.

Melodie chose to pretend it hadn't happened at all, only saying, "That explains why it was so hard getting back to the hotel when I first came here. There was a rock… You can't see it now. I guess the tide is higher, but I had to sit and catch my breath. I was so sorry I didn't have a camera, though—"

"Wait, what are you talking about? You swam in that current? When?" He turned into robot Roman, the one who shot out questions, extracting information like a laser scalpel, green eyes piercing into hers.

"That day. The last time I was here." Maybe that was why she was picking a fight. The tension of coming back to this place was adding to the uncertainty she felt in their relationship.

"There are signs that say No Swimming."

"I know, but I was hot and tired and my feet hurt. I wasn't wearing shoes. Swimming across the bay looked shorter than walking all the way around, so—"

"I sent a cab, Melodie! I told them to find you on the road and assumed they did. Are you seriously telling me you swam in that?" He pointed toward the streak of white foam.

"I swam across it. Not in it. I'm not stupid."

"I beg to differ!" His voice went up. "People die in this area every year. Stupid tourists who think they're strong enough to— *What the hell were you thinking?*"

"That I wanted to get back to the hotel." She'd seen Roman angry before, especially that first day, but nothing like this. He wasn't just irritated. There was a quality beneath his flush of rage that hinted at desperation. She could see him fighting for control, visibly struggling, but his temper exploded out of him anyway.

"You could have died!" he shouted. The curses that followed weren't exactly aimed at her, but they had enough color to take her aback.

She stared, wide-eyed in astonishment as he paced away a few feet, looked across the water, slammed another look her direction that was so outraged it should have knocked her overboard, then smacked his fist onto the rail.

"Don't you *ever* do anything so reckless again. Do you hear me? No matter how sad you are about losing your mother or how angry you are at me, you do *not* act as if your life means nothing. You're smarter than that. You're—" He pressed his finger and thumb into his eye sockets, shoulders bowing for a moment. "The world needs more people like you. Don't act as though you're disposable."

He threw himself away from the rail and disappeared into the interior of the yacht.

Melodie realized that the weight on her neck was her camera. Her hands had gone lax at her sides. Thank goodness she always kept it tethered or it would be on the bottom of the sea by now.

She swallowed, stunned by the depth of emotion that had just detonated out of Roman in a way she could never have expected. It took her a few minutes to recover from her shock, but she finally did and went to find him.

He was in his office, door firmly locked against intrusion.

CHAPTER ELEVEN

ROMAN FELT LIKE an idiot—one of his least favorite feelings. Although he'd already been standing there feeling it before he'd behaved like a mother hen on steroids.

Melodie had been right. A part of him had been convinced she wouldn't last until the wedding, that his aloof persona would drive her away and he'd be without a date at all when the big day happened.

Instead, she'd become such an integral part of his world he feared he couldn't live without her. As she'd made her facetious little remarks today, he'd heard the hurt beneath. Maybe other women had been as injured by his reserve, but he hadn't felt an answering pinch in the same way. He hadn't hated himself quite as much for causing suffering. He hadn't considered explaining that being nothing more than a file all your life, having your personal details handed from one person to the next, as if privacy was for other people, not you, had left a mark.

Maybe if those details hadn't made it from the confidentiality of a folder into the mouths of his foster home siblings, he could have withstood it, but the foster parents had always managed to gossip somewhere along the line and the kids had always wound up overhearing. Then the hierarchy of judgment would start. Kids who were abused were rescues. Kids such as him, whose parents were deemed reprehensible, were tarred as worthless.

Oddly, with Melodie he already knew she wouldn't

make those same judgments. But it was the very fact that she wouldn't, and would more likely try to comfort him, that made it seem an even more painful prospect to open up to her.

So he'd stood there trying to see a way out of the corner he'd painted himself into when she'd distracted him by telling him what she'd done after leaving him that day. After she'd fled like a Victorian maiden ravished by the local duke. Hot, tired, emotionally distressed, she'd done something so irresponsible he could hardly think of it.

Every summer the local news reported on at least one or two deaths in that current. The fact the tide had kept the water low was likely the only thing that had kept her from being a headline and statistic. His blood ran icy thinking of it.

The vibration of the engine stilled. They were at the dock outside his home. No more hiding. He pulled out his earbuds, ceasing to pretend he was working, and gathered himself to face Melodie. Hell, the entire crew had probably heard him tear a strip off her and would stare at him.

He wasn't entirely sorry. She *had* been heedless of very real danger, but he was angry with himself, too, for raising his voice. She was sensitive, her thoughts and feelings so easy to read he couldn't help but trust her.

But he was furious with himself for letting emotion get the best of him. He'd ceased trying to figure out why she prompted such strong feelings in him. All he could do was work to control and hide them.

He cursed under his breath, ran a hand over his face to clear his expression and unlocked the door.

It wouldn't have surprised him to find Melodie packing to leave him, and she *was* in his cabin loosely gathering some things that she'd piled on the bed, but she'd stopped to look at her camera. Her hair hung in a loose curtain off one side of her bent head, her lips were pouted into concentration, her thumb working the controls while the rest of her slender height was still.

He couldn't count the number of times he'd found her like this since he'd bought the thing for her. She loved it, and Roman got a kick of amusement and pleasure every time he saw how much she enjoyed it. Her photos were excellent and she was always fooling around with the settings, reviewing what she'd done, trying to improve. He did the same with his own work and liked seeing her pursue something that gave her so much satisfaction.

"I was worried that you were dragging your feet about telling Ingrid because you weren't sure if you really wanted me here," she murmured without looking up, reminding him that the radar between them worked both ways. He rarely sneaked up on her without getting a smile of greeting before he was in touching distance.

No smile today. She didn't even look at him.

"I couldn't assume you'd want to be here, not after the way I treated you the first time we were in this house together." He had barely admitted that to himself and didn't like saying it aloud. He didn't revenge to remind her. She might agree and leave.

Then, even though it made him feel as obvious as a boy picking flowers, he gave her what he thought she needed to hear.

"And I have never invited any woman here, except you and Ingrid that day. I suppose it sounds ridiculous that I had to think about it when you've already been here, but I wanted to be sure I was making the right choice, bringing you into my home." It had been a remarkably easy decision, in fact. So easy he'd forced himself to mull it over, refusing to commit until the last minute despite his gut clamoring for her to become a fixture there.

She finally looked up, her blue gaze surprised and vulnerable, searched his in a way that made him deeply uncomfortable because he feared he didn't have whatever it was she was hoping to find. He had to look away first, which was a terribly revealing thing to do, but he couldn't take her scrutiny.

She set her camera on the bed before coming across to him, expression solemn. When she cupped the side of his face, his first instinct was to tense with resistance. She ignored his rebuff and lifted on tiptoes to set her lips against the corner of his mouth.

"Thank you for telling me that," she said, breath warm against his lips and chin.

As her scent filled his nostrils and she started to lower to flat feet, his arms went around her of their own accord. He felt her start, then soften to accept the convulsive tightening of his arms around her.

Words, stupid words, crowded his throat, but he couldn't put them in any sort of order that made sense. He couldn't figure out which ones were safe to say and which ones would hurt and damage and lower her opinion of him. He could only frown at the carpet over her shoulder and drink in her scent, cheek to cheek with her.

Somewhere beyond the door, one of the crew said something about luggage. Footsteps approached and Roman and Melodie stepped apart.

An hour later, when the crew had dispersed to beach-based pursuits and the house was theirs alone, he caught up to Melodie in his master bedroom. She was in the walk-in closet, hanging a dress she'd obviously decided would be suitable for the wedding tomorrow.

He turned her toward him again, unable to keep from kissing her. He wanted her. Needed to make love to her. Not with the passion and lust of their first time, but with this well of tender cherishing overflowing within him. Soft feelings like gratitude and deep admiration filled him so thoroughly he had to pour them onto her, to somehow communicate how deeply he regarded her.

It was so intense they could only lie in silence afterward, bodies tangled, damp skin glued as if only a fragile cell wall kept them from conjoining into one being. He should have been disturbed by the magnitude of the moment, but he was oddly reassured. They fell asleep with the filmy white curtains shifting in the light breeze, the swish of low waves hypnotic and lulling.

The next morning Ingrid aimed a very pointed look at Melodie the moment she entered the house. The day already had got off to an extremely busy start with people arriving every five minutes. The wedding planners hired to replace Melodie were a male-female duo who were competent enough, but wound up with so many questions Melodie might as well have been the one organizing it all.

She had quietly appointed herself in charge rather than pressing Roman into that position. If *she* asked him whether a tent should be moved twelve feet, he gave the matter serious consideration. If anyone else asked him for an opinion, he gave them a look that suggested they take a long walk off his short dock.

So Melodie was running interference—even when she wound up in the guest room with his former PA, the bride-to-be.

"How—?" Ingrid blurted as she opened a small suitcase that was all makeup, hairbrushes, curling irons and body glitter.

"There was a misunderstanding. We worked it out," Melodie said with a circumspect smile, not pretending she didn't know what Ingrid was asking.

"Oh, Melodie," Ingrid said with a pitiful shake of her head. "You've turned out just like him. Are you really not going to give me any of the details?"

"Maybe another time," she lied. "When you're not so busy. Surely you have better things to do today? The salon people have taken over the sitting room. Let me get a round of mimosas for you and the bridal party. I'll meet you in there."

The day came together beautifully. When Ingrid came down the stairs she was a vision, making the entire guest list gasp in unison. Lilies floated in the pool, carpet lining her route alongside it, but she still sent a wink toward Melodie as she made it past the hazard without mishap. She met Huxley under the archway set up for the occasion, and their vows and deep connection brought tears to Melodie's eyes.

Tears of happiness, but sad ones, too. That kind of everlasting commitment to another person was her dream, but she wasn't holding her breath that it would ever really happen. Roman cared for her. She was convinced of that much after his freak-out over her swim in the rip current, but he didn't feel anything like what Ingrid and Huxley shared. Not the kind of love that demanded to be locked in for a lifetime.

She distracted herself by playing back-up photographer, surprised when she heard a masculine and intimate "Hey, beautiful."

Looking up with a smile already in her eyes, she found herself confronted with Roman's phone. It clicked and he lowered it.

"Did you seriously just take my photo?"

"I did. And don't you dare aim yours at me. Put it down and come dance with me."

"Since you asked so nicely," she teased, wrinkling her nose at him, but pouting a little that he was dodging a photo. He was in a tuxedo. That was always a good look for him.

She loved dancing with him, though. They were a perfect match height-wise, and he led with smooth assurance. "Are you a natural? Or did you take lessons?" she found herself asking.

A pause, then, "Lessons seemed a wise investment once I began attending formal events."

She let that fact absorb, along with the knowledge that Roman hadn't hesitated very long at all before answering a personal question. Perhaps they were making progress.

"Are you enjoying this formal occasion? You were rather pithy about weddings the first time we talked.

"No," he answered, his reply so prompt she flashed a glance upward at him.

A pang of disappointment struck. He still found weddings a waste of time, then.

"I wish they'd all go home so I could have you to myself," he said. "You really do look incredible. That shade of blue is definitely your color, and those shoes are coming to bed with us."

She laughed, enjoying his suggestive remark and the reassurance that it wasn't the wedding putting that dismayed edge in his voice.

"Whatever possessed you to invite four hundred people into your home if you hate weddings so much?" she asked.

He didn't answer and she sighed inwardly, thinking they'd lost that fragile strand of communication twining them together. It was always like this, and it created a lot of despair in her.

"I'm embarrassed to tell you," he said so quietly she almost didn't hear him.

She tried not to betray how surprised she was, just murmured, "Why? It's a very nice thing to do."

"If it was for Ingrid's sake, it would be, but I wanted people—her sort of people—to see me as their equal. Now they're here, I can't be bothered speaking to them. I'd rather dance with you." His mouth quirked in self-derision.

The importance of status was never lost on someone with a family in politics, but Melodie heard something else in his tone. Humbleness. *Her sort of people.*

"You are their equal," she informed him with quiet sincerity.

"I told you what kind of mother I had."

"One who made sacrifices for her child. Trust me. You do not own the patent on scandal or tragedy. I would think a man who makes his living running background checks would be fully aware of that."

Roman had to hand it to her. Each time he gathered his courage and revealed a moment of personal angst, she came through, reminding him that he had every reason to stand tall.

They made the rounds after that, branching out from the bride's and groom's immediate family, whom they'd already met, to circulate among the other guests. Melodie fairly sparkled, she was so bright and delightful. He even found himself laughing when she described her fall into the pool that first day, only excusing them when someone joked that Roman had pushed her so he could perform mouth-to-mouth.

"I'm sorry," Melodie murmured as he steered her toward the bar.

"It's not your fault," he said. "The guy is drunk." And it was juvenile of him to feel insulted and mocked, but he didn't want anyone to think he treated women roughly. He was past throwing punches over that sort of thing, but he didn't listen to it. As for being so smitten with Melodie he would behave like a dolt in a romantic comedy, well, he wasn't about to stand around for that accusation, either.

In all honesty, the whole day was a bit of a trial for Roman on that score, constantly demanding that he examine his feelings and intentions toward her. In fact, he had watched Huxley gaze at Ingrid in a way that wasn't far off from what he was beginning to feel toward Melodie. She was precious and beautiful and captivating to him, but he couldn't bring himself to tell her or allow others to see that in him.

"I'm going to take a few more photos," she murmured, touching his arm as she stepped away.

He nodded, aware he could call her back, that she probably wanted him to, but letting her go anyway. He didn't wear his emotions on his sleeve. He didn't even know how to put on the coat.

CHAPTER TWELVE

MELODIE UNDERSTOOD NOW. She wasn't tired of Roman, but a woman could take only so much uncertainty. She kept telling herself to live in the moment, enjoy what they had, that taking it day by day was fine. She didn't delude herself that there was another man out there who had all Roman's qualities plus an open heart, a desire for commitment and a burning need for children. The man she was with was definitely as perfect as she could expect.

But not knowing how long she and Roman would last made her anxious. She was always looking for the end so she could anticipate it, soften the blow. She could easily see why his other companions had made it happen just to get the suspense over with.

She didn't want to leave him, though. She loved him.

Loved him, loved him, loved him.

And if she judged him on his actions, he cared quite deeply for her. At least that was what she thought he was communicating. So when she received a job offer, Melodie was torn.

Under any other circumstance she would have been beyond elated by the contents of the email, but it meant leaving Roman for a few days. That made it a bit of a test of their relationship. On the other hand, it gave her the fallback position she needed if they were destined to break up.

The prospect of confronting exactly how tenuous their

relationship was kept her silent on the topic for several days, until she *had* to make a decision or lose the opportunity altogether.

She brought it up over breakfast in the sunroom she adored.

"It's an Italian couple. Well, the wife is Canadian. They're friends with the Marcussens and saw the photos I'd taken of the family. They asked if I'd come to their home on Lake Como and take some candid shots of them with their children. It would have to be next week," she said, trying not to betray how nervous she was.

Roman set aside his tablet and sat back in his chair. He wore his usual morning attire of pajama pants, so he was all bare-chested and manly. She wore the silk robe he'd bought her in Paris. A morning breeze wafted in, dewy and tanged by the lemon grove. The low, quiet murmur of waves on the shore was the only sound for a long moment.

"I have to be in New York." No inflection. No real reaction beyond exchanging information.

"I know. That's why I'm talking to you about it. I keep trying to say no, and they keep offering me more money. They'll pay for my flight, put me up. They're very determined, but it has to be next week or it won't happen at all."

"Do you want to do it?"

She lifted a shoulder, genuinely conflicted. Roman could call her his companion all he wanted, but she knew she was his mistress. As idyllic as it should have felt to let him support her, she had spent a lot of years becoming self-reliant. She might not *need* a job right now, but she *wanted* one, and being a photographer was a dream career for her, something she'd barely imagined she could pursue as a hobby, let alone anything more. If she could establish herself at this level, it could be a proper way to make a living.

"It's a really good opportunity," she managed to say.

"You told me I could be a professional if I took money for my photos, and this couple seems to think I'm good enough. I guess there is a part of me that wants to try."

Nothing showed on his face. Only his green eyes flickered as he cataloged every nuance of her expression, making her feel more self-conscious by the second. Was she fooling herself? Was she really not that good?

Did it bother him at all that she was talking about leaving? That she wouldn't be at his beck and call?

"This could turn into a career for you," he said.

"I keep thinking it could, yes." She glanced at the hands in her lap that were knotting her belt, trying to disguise the disappointment that he hadn't first leaped to how it would affect him. *Them.* "I don't have any illusions," she continued, doing the work for him so he'd see the broader picture. "I realize I'd be chasing commissions and have to do a lot of traveling."

She flicked a look up at him.

Still nothing. Her heart felt pinched in a vice that slowly closed as she squeezed out what she thought needed to be said.

"That's something I always wanted to do. Travel." It was his cue to say, "We already travel." He didn't.

"Running your own business isn't a picnic, I know," she continued. "I don't even know where I'd pay taxes or if I need a work visa, but…"

"You'd regret it if you didn't try," he summed up. He was very still, very watchful, but didn't express any regret on his side. This was purely her decision, he seemed to be saying.

"I think I would, yes." She said the words steadily enough, but her heart was listing in her chest. Sinking.

He nodded. "Then, you should do whatever you need to. I have every confidence that you could be very successful if you give it your all. I won't hold you back."

His words were like the slide of a guillotine, hissing and thunking. She'd known this moment would happen, but the shock still reverberated through her. It was over. She had wanted him to fight for her, but he was making it easy for her to leave him. She nodded, head loose on her shoulders. "I'll go email them."

She rose, feeling weightless and uncoordinated. Despite the warmth of the morning, her skin pimpled with cold. Her fingers were nerveless and her essence stayed at the table while the shell of her body moved away.

The separation of soul and self was so painful she couldn't even react. Couldn't cry.

When Roman made love to her that night she shuddered in ecstasy but couldn't talk afterward. Couldn't face the emptiness of her future, even though emptiness was the only option open to her.

If she had thought there was a chance for them, she might have forgone taking the job and stayed with him, but Roman wasn't like her. He enjoyed female company, loved sex, cared to a point, but he didn't love her back.

And maybe, if she hadn't seen firsthand how emotional and financial dependence had gutted her mother's self-esteem, Melodie might have settled for one-sided love. But she couldn't do that to herself.

So she held back her tears until, a handful of days later, Roman left for New York and she caught a flight to Italy. They pretended they'd see each other soon, but she knew this was the beginning of the end. Better to make the break a clean one.

Before Melodie had even finished her work in Italy and sent her thank-you note to the Marcussens for referring her, she received a request from each of Nic's three siblings asking her to do similar jobs for them. Without hesitation she accepted the commissions. She found herself in Athens by the end of that week, Paris the next and over to New York at the end of the month.

Roman was gone from that city by then, having been called to a supplier's factory in China. Their face-to-face wireless connections had turned into texts and emails and became more sporadic. She had thought—hoped—Roman would make the effort to track her down or invite her to meet him somewhere, but her schedule was constantly filling and he was making no effort to ask her to come back to him.

Their temporary separation had obviously clarified itself into the natural end to their arrangement. It felt like an amputation. She pined and longed and yearned. Fortunately, though, she was so busy she could only break down at night before she went to sleep alone and dreamed she was with him again.

At least she was creating a decent life for herself. As word spread, a studio in New York reached out to her. It was extremely well respected, had all the print facilities and lined up gigs for its photographers. Quite unexpectedly, Melodie had a home base in the city she'd always wanted to inhabit. All her preparations for the wedding-planning business came in handy now as she reworked them for her new photography business. Practically overnight she was supporting herself.

Roman greased the wheels, of course. She realized that after a few weeks, when one of the studio owners dropped a remark about how he'd come to hear of her. The sublease on her one-room flat was equally a convenient find, but she chose not to fight Roman on it. She suspected he was trying to make up for flattening her first attempt at a

proper career. She let him help her. It was a kindness that
went both ways.

But she missed him with every breath in her body, every
minute of every day.

Roman was stunned. It took him weeks to fully absorb
that Melodie had left him. One day he was waking to the
shift of silken limbs against him, the next he was walking around like a bomb-blast victim, shell-shocked and
unable to make sense of the empty landscape around him.

He kept going back to that moment when she'd told him
she had a job offer. He had felt everything in him drain-
ing away then. He'd seen himself about to lose everything
and he hadn't known how to stop it. It was like being nine
years old again, completely powerless to change what was
happening to him.

He couldn't stand in the way of Melodie taking a job
she wanted, though. He'd already caused her to lose her
livelihood twice. And she genuinely loved photography.
How could he blurt out that the idea of her leaving him
made him physically sick?

Which was the real crux of the matter, he knew. He
hadn't had the courage even to face how deep the cut
went as she was carved out of his life. The bleeding never
seemed to let up. He barely slept, having no desire to crawl
into an empty bed, and when he woke he saw no point in
rising. His company was dominating the financial pages.
The demise of Gautier Enterprises was a done deal. They
were declaring bankruptcy while rumors of corruption
dogged its board. He couldn't care less.

His schedule had finally pulled him to New York, where
he knew Melodie now had a flat, but she wasn't even in
the city. He followed her social-media accounts, and she
was posting from Spain.

A blip on the reader of his office door announced his

PA, Colette. He liked her well enough now that she was up to speed. Ingrid had always been cheerfully efficient, and Colette was equally strong on details and light in mood, not that anything really penetrated anymore. If he had felt like a puppet before, someone who moved through life without feeling, now he felt like a ghost. Even simple sensory pleasures such as a good meal or a piece of music were lost on him.

The worst part was he had fought deep emotions for so long he ought to have been an expert at suppressing them. The things he was feeling now were too big, however. Too dark and heavy and all pervading. There was no escaping the barbed and piercing pain that squeezed him in its coil.

He was in hell.

"Lunch," Colette said, holding up a white bag, snapping him from what he realized had become a blank stare. "Thanks for buying this round. Everyone is really grateful."

He shrugged. Colette had started a Friday lunch thing that seemed to boost morale and communication. She'd invited him to join them, but Roman had declined, preferring to brood in here alone.

He would always be alone.

He should have asked Melodie to stay.

But he couldn't. Not when she deserved so much more than he was able to offer her.

Colette left, and he moved with robotic detachment, pulling out the carton and finding Chinese markings on its side. He wasn't hungry for anything, he realized, least of all cheap noodles and overly sauced, chewy meat.

But he supposed he should eat.

Fishing for the chopsticks, he wound up touching something that he recognized and almost didn't want to see, but he pulled it out and looked at it anyway: a fortune cookie.

He'd met Melodie many months ago, had spent countless hours with her since, and still he could remember their first conversation. She'd been so disappointed in him, so brightly engaging with her optimism in the way she described marriage, while he'd called weddings a shell for a useless piece of paper.

Before he realized what he was doing to do, rage broke through his shields and he smashed the cookie, pulverizing it in its cellophane wrapper. The white fortune with its pink ink peeked through beige shrapnel.

Swearing, wondering how the hell his control had deserted him so thoroughly, he opened the package and shook out the crumbs until he could pick out the tiny strip of paper.

"Patience will be rewarded sooner or later."

Had he really hoped for actual guidance? Fortune cookies were stupid.

Weddings and marriage and lifetime commitments were equally useless things to place faith in. Just like women were.

Moving to the window, Roman rubbed a knuckle against his brow, chest tight. Was that what he really thought? That women were faithless? Because his mother had died before she could get him back? Because every woman he'd remotely cared about had left?

Had he given any of them a reason to stay?

The fact was, his father had been the one to abandon his mother. What did it say about Roman that he hadn't even tried to keep Melodie in his life? Did there have to be a child at risk for *him* to take a risk? What made anyone fight to keep someone in their life?

On impulse, he turned to the phone and dialed a number he knew by heart, but rarely called. The woman who answered was the only woman he'd ever known who'd completely devoted herself to one man, despite the fact he'd left her—involuntarily, but definitely left her—years ago.

"Brenda? It's Roman. Can I buy you lunch?"

A surprised pause, then, "Why don't you come over here? I'll make you grilled cheese."

Grilled cheese and tomato soup. Hardly the fine dining he'd grown used to, but Roman was ridiculously comforted by the simple meal when he sat down in Brenda's kitchen an hour later in what had been his only real home, and even then only for a year.

Brenda, so motherly it had been almost unbearable when he'd lived here, poured him a glass of milk, still attempting to nurture him. He hated milk. Always had, probably because he'd drunk it sour more times than not.

"This is a really lovely surprise, Roman." She stopped there, didn't ask him why he was here, even though her curiosity was evident in the long silence after she spoke. But she understood him and respected his boundaries. He'd always appreciated that about her.

So even though he felt like a world-class idiot, he opened his chest and set his heart on the table, self-deprecatingly stating, "I'm having girl trouble, Brenda."

"And you came to me? I'm touched, Roman. I truly am. Tell me about her."

He stalled. How could he possibly describe Melodie and all she'd come to mean to him? Her smiles, her quiet toughness, her fierce resiliency and her soft, soft heart.

"I just want to know…what makes people stick around? Is there something I can say that would make her come back? For good? Because I'm not good with words and…"

She wasn't laughing at him. Her graying head was bent a little as she patiently watched him struggle.

"Charles doesn't recognize you anymore, but you're with him as much as you can be. What keeps you faithful?" he asked.

She flinched, then smiled crookedly. "*He* does."

Roman narrowed his eyes, trying to understand.

Brenda lowered her gaze to stir her soup. "I've always kept Charles's confidences, but I can see you need to hear some of them. He told me once, not long after he hired you, that he saw something of himself in you. That always made me sad because I knew what he'd been through as a child. His mother had a boyfriend who was very cruel to him. Very, very cruel." Her voice hollowed. "I know he didn't even tell me all of it, but what he did tell me…" She shook her head. "I don't know how people can be like that to another human being."

Roman's view of his first employer, a man who'd been athletic and smart and gruffly wise—seemingly impervious—shifted. He grew angry on his friend's behalf. He wanted to go back in time and defend this person he'd suddenly discovered he not only respected and admired, but cared about very much.

"It wasn't easy in our early days. He simply didn't want to talk. I completely understand that coping strategy. I don't want to talk about how difficult it is to put the man I love in a home and watch his health decline. To see him every day but never see recognition in his eyes." She welled up and dabbed a napkin to her trembling lips, recovering her composure after a moment. "Some things are just too painful to speak about."

"Brenda, what can I do?" he said, reaching out impulsively. It wasn't like him at all, but he'd gotten into the habit of touching Melodie when she was upset, trying to comfort, and his affection for Brenda ran as deep.

"You've done all that can be done. Research," she said with a fatalistic lift of her shoulder. "Hopefully in the future it won't come to this for other spouses and families. But what I'm trying to say is that I understand how futile it feels to speak about things that can't be changed."

He nodded. That was it exactly. Why bother telling Melodie that he'd once nearly been raped, that he had a cigar burn scar under his elbow or how alone he'd felt after his mother had died? What point would it serve?

"But talking helps," Brenda said quietly, adding with an apologetic smile, "Talking is important, Roman. Especially to a woman. Charles showed me in a million ways that he loved me, but until he said the words, I wasn't sure. And once he'd said it, once we'd devoted ourselves to each other, I knew that nothing could separate us. His illness makes it impossible for him to show me he still loves me, but I know he does. It would break his heart if I stopped believing it… But I wouldn't know how much he loved me if he hadn't told me before his illness started affecting him."

Roman winced from that peek into the intimacy of his friends' marriage. And he cringed from the idea of laying his heart on the line so blatantly. What if Melodie didn't want his love? Yes, he knew she wanted the whole package, but what if she'd left because she'd rather someone else offered it?

They finished eating in silence, but afterward he took out his phone and showed Brenda his gallery of Melodie photos, from springtime in Paris to her languid smiles on his yacht to the dreamy beauty of two days before she'd left him, when he'd caught her on the beach, taking a break from using her own camera to lift her face to the sun.

"Is there a reason you're sitting in an old lady's kitchen rather than chasing this woman down?" Brenda asked. "A picture is worth a thousand words, and there are a million 'I love yous' in each of those photos."

His heart lurched. He stood, smirking to hide how desperately he hoped she was right. Touching her shoulder, he wavered, then gave in to impulse and bent to kiss her cheek. Then, because he was starting to understand how this worked, he said, "Your generosity has always meant the world to me, Brenda. You're like a second mother to me. I wish I'd let you treat me like your son."

It was a terrible risk that paid off immediately.

"Oh, my boy." She patted his hand and turned her face to kiss his knuckles. "There's still time to let me. Invite me to your wedding."

CHAPTER THIRTEEN

MELODIE WONDERED IF there was anything quite so beautiful as an Indian wedding. She'd covered a few nuptials by now, including an Arab one that had been so over-the-top with luxury she'd been fairly sure she'd been transported to another planet. This one in London, where both families lived, had a celebratory quality that was as solid and fascinating as the abundant gold weighing down the bride. The colors, dear Lord, the colors. And when it came to capturing the joy of family and children—something that was becoming her forte—there was nothing so perfect as the natural warmth of two Indian families coming together through a love match.

Maybe it was the cultural shift that made her appreciate this wedding more than the Spanish heiress's last week. That one had made it too easy for to see herself in the gown and Roman in the morning coat. It had left her crying hard through the night. She couldn't think of it now. She'd start crying again.

Roman was gone. Life had to go on.

She forced her mind back to arranging the groom's family, with his parents and abundance of siblings, their spouses and children, along with his new bride. One of the four-year-olds in the party had pretty much given up on this exercise, so Melodie had to snap fast.

"No, please, keep looking at the camera," she called when half of the arrangement turned their heads to take note of something across the room. Beautiful, happy people abounded at weddings, but when the groups got this big, it was like herding cats to get them all to do one thing.

They weren't cooperating. The distraction of the growing reception was too much. The groom actually stepped away to meet someone working through the crowd. The rest of the group broke up. Melodie silently whimpered, then felt a tingle that she usually only felt when—

She gasped and spun around at the exact moment she heard, "I need to speak to your photographer."

Roman. So tall, so commanding. So inappropriately dressed in a T-shirt and jeans, a brown leather jacket thrown on over it.

"What are you doing here?" she asked, voice squeaking with astonishment. Her body actually hurt from the sting of excitement that shot through her veins.

"I want to talk to you."

"How did you even find me?" She'd been called in last minute on this one, flying to London first thing this morning.

"Your office. They owed me for referring you in the first place. I didn't realize you'd be working." He gave the anxious bride a friendly nod. "I don't know why it didn't occur to me. Weddings are evening events, so the odds were good, I suppose. But I won't get you fired." He turned to the groom, handed over his card and said something about a free security system for a home or office if he was allowed to borrow Melodie for a few minutes.

"Can we go somewhere?" he said to Melodie, taking her arm and looking over the heads in the crowd, starting to usher her from the ballroom toward the interior of the hotel.

"Where? No," she added quickly when he signaled to a

server in a uniform. "No hotel room. You know what will happen and I *will* get fired."

He acknowledged that with a cant of his head and a quirk of his lips. "Promising," he remarked under his breath, changing direction toward a door to the balcony.

"Also, I'm not pregnant, if that's why you're here," she blurted, unable to think of another reason.

He opened his mouth, paused, then said, "We'll come back to that one."

Would they? Her heart was already going a mile a minute, and now it threatened to leave her body altogether.

He drew her away from the wedding guests milling on the balcony and moved toward the outdoor café that was shut down for the evening, sectioned off at the far side. He scissored his legs over the low glass rail that separated the area while she moved into the shadows and opened the gate, letting herself in. They circled around a trellis and moved to where they could see the Thames cutting through the sparkle of city lights.

And there her world stopped, because it was all she could do to hold back a choke of tears, she was so happy to see him and so devastated at the same time. Did he have any idea how difficult it would be to say goodbye again?

It was up to her to talk, though, she supposed, and searched for her voice, wanting to know why he really was here.

He surprised her by saying abruptly, "It wasn't just the way your father and brother treated me." The words dropped into the empty air off the top of the hotel. His hands gripped the rail and he didn't look at her. "It was the same message again and again my whole life. My needs weren't important. My feelings didn't matter. No one cared, so what was the point in showing or asking or wanting? It was far easier to become self-sufficient and not talk to anyone."

It was such an odd yet intimate statement, she could only stare up at him, shocked and rather suspecting he'd been rehearsing the words, waiting to get them off his chest.

Her hand went to his and he quickly turned his palm up to grasp her fingers, making her blood sing. The pressure was so tight it was just this side of painful, warning her that for all the detachment he was affecting, this was very hard for him. But still he was trying. Reaching out. Asking to be understood.

"I learned to shut myself off, too," she offered. "When I was surrounded by people who watched to see what was important to me so they could use it against me. I would never try to hurt you like that, Roman. I hope you believe that."

"I do. That's why..." In the dark, she saw him struggle to retain his stoic expression.

When he didn't continue and the only sound became the music that grew louder as doors were opened off the ballroom, she covered his grip in a signal to ease up his hold. "Roman, why are you here?" she asked, pushing the words past the catch in her throat.

"I never saw any point in marriage," he said, continuing to squish her fingers while she went lax in his grip, not wanting to hear the tiny sparks of her dream snuffed out for good.

"Then I realized that if you were my wife, and you knew I expected you to come back after each job, maybe you would."

"Oh, my God," she whispered, feeling as if this tight grip of theirs was the only thing keeping her from plummeting off the building.

"I want to love you, Melodie, but I don't know if I know how. I quit feeling anything years ago to save myself pain. I fought what I feel for you as hard as I could, but I can't *not* feel something for you. And I don't know whether it's enough. Is it love? I don't know. I just know it's…good. When I think of you, when I touch you, the way I feel is so damned good. Sweet and hopeful and warm—all the things you are. I lose all that when you're not with me. It's just hollow emptiness and I can't stand it. It *hurts*. Every day. I want the good feeling back. I want *you* back."

Her head spun. Her heart soared on a roller coaster, climbing and dipping and spiraling so she didn't know which way was up.

"All the way here a voice in my head kept telling me you wouldn't forgive me for letting you go in the first place. I was afraid I'd broken you again, that you'd stopped believing in men and love and the sort of life you deserve. But…" He reached his free hand into his shirt pocket and came up with something small.

A shiny black pearl nestled against a shiny white one in a platinum setting surrounded by glittering diamonds. She was sure she was going to faint at that point. Or she was dreaming and would wake up. Could this possibly be real?

"How's that for optimism?" he said. "The minute I saw it, I thought of you." He started to kneel.

"Oh, Roman, no!"

He froze. "You don't—?"

She felt his recoil at the perceived rejection and threw herself against his stiff body. "No, I mean, yes! I want to marry you. I love you. You don't have to go down on one knee!"

His breath rushed out and his arms tightened on her. "Sweetheart. This is one of the few romantic gestures I could possibly figure out on my own. Let me do it." He gently set her back a step, a half grin catching at the corner of his mouth as he went down on one knee. "Saved me some suspense, at least. Will you marry me, Melodie Parnell?"

He offered the ring and she found her throat too locked to speak again. All she could do was nod and hold out her shaking hand. He threaded the ring onto her finger and she fell on him, letting him catch her on his hard thigh and squeeze her to his brawny chest with viselike arms so tight she could barely breathe except to gasp, "Yes."

"And you love me? Because if you're not sure—"

"I do," she said, sniffing back emotional tears that refused to stay behind her eyes. "Believe me, I've tried not to, but I love you so much I feel as if I'm dying without you. I *was* angry you let me go," she admitted. "But since you came after me, I'll forgive you."

"So softhearted," he murmured, brushing his lips against her temple. "I'm sorry I didn't tell you that day that your leaving was the worst possible thing you could ever do to me. I didn't know how to stop you. I couldn't find the words and, damn it, Melodie. I had destroyed your livelihood twice. I know how much you love photography. How could I refuse to let you try to make a career of it?"

"I do love photography. Just not as much as I love you," she pouted, clinging to his neck as he lifted her and moved them both into a chair, her on his lap, legs dangling over the arm. She couldn't get close enough. Each cell in her body plumped a little more with each breath, like a succulent absorbing the water it needed to survive.

He breathed a laugh against her hairline. "You have no idea how much I like hearing you say that."

"That I love you? I do!" She hugged him again. "But I don't want to quit working," she rushed to say. "Not altogether. Just, you know, I won't let it come between us again."

"That's okay. I would never ask you to give up something you enjoy so much. But, yes, if you could ease up, maybe take fewer clients so we can have more time together, I'd like that a lot. Charge more," he advised loftily.

"A lot more. Slow down those offers and make it worth our while for you to leave our bed."

She snorted, wanting to be in bed with him right now. He wanted that, too. She could feel him hard against her hip and wriggled to let him know they were on the same page. That part hadn't changed one teensy bit, and she missed him *so much*.

He stilled her with firm hands. "Darling, you know where that's going to lead. I'll be arrested along with getting you fired."

"Might be worth it," she teased, nipping at his jaw.

"Might be," he agreed, running possessive hands over her. "But maybe it's a good thing that I don't have the option of letting my body do the talking right now. It's not easy for me to open up. For you, for us, I want to try, though. No one has ever affected me the way you do, Melodie. From the first moment… Hell, I am the last person to believe in love at first sight or soul mates, but no one means as much to me as you do."

She swallowed and ducked her forehead under his jaw, too moved to speak.

"I want to change, to be whatever it is you need in a man, but it will be hard. Bear with me. That's all I'm asking," he said, cradling the back of her head in his big hand. "And maybe, after we've given ourselves some time, if you want…" He swallowed, then cleared his throat. "We could talk about a baby. If you want."

She tightened her arms around his neck and shuddered as a sob of joy took her.

"Don't cry. I said only if you want," he rushed to repeat.

"I'm happy!" she choked. "You're giving me everything I ever wanted. I can't help crying."

"Oh," he said ruefully, cuddling her closer. "Okay." He took a deep, emotive breath that shook her on his chest. "I want to make you happy."

"You do," she assured him. "Just by being with me. I love you."

"Is that how it works? Because it's the same for me," he said, tilting his head and tipping hers so they could look into each other's eyes. "I was missing you as though a piece of me was gone. Then, the minute I saw you today, everything was right. I need you in my life to make it worth living. That must be love, right?"

"I'm sure of it," she agreed, pressing her smile to his.

EPILOGUE

MELODIE STEPPED OUT to the glitter of evening sunlight bouncing off the sea. As she reached the top of the stairs, the silk of her gown poured like milk off the first step.

She paused to gather it, sending a smile to her groom where he waited at the bottom.

Roman wore a black tuxedo with a cream-colored waistcoat and a silk tie in the same color. It was the perfect level of formality for their small wedding and, as usual, it didn't matter what he wore. He projected masculine beauty no matter what.

He leaped up the steps to take her bouquet and offer his free hand, ensuring she was steady as she made her way down. No father of the bride to give her away. She hadn't even considered it, thankful that her "memoir" and her brother's financial and legal troubles had kept both her father and Anton out of their lives for good.

No, Roman was walking with her to their understated altar. He hadn't wanted to wait for her to come to him on the beach. *The whole point of marriage is to do things together, isn't it?* he'd said as they were making the plans.

So she'd been allowed to kick him out of their bedroom while she put on her gown, but that was it. They'd even slept together last night, making love and murmuring their "I love yous" afterward just as they did every night. He said it again now, as they started to walk.

Her heart swelled, moved every time he spoke those particular words, but feeling them especially today.

"I love you, too," she breathed.

Floating candles barely moved as they passed the pool, flames burning steadily. Overhead, the sky was deepening from a pink glow to a devoted red. Potted flowers perfumed the warm air, giving her a vague déjà vu feeling, as if she remembered this moment from another life.

They reached the beach and the carpet where their guests stood waiting. It was a small wedding with only a few of her friends from Virginia and two colleagues from New York. Roman had invited a handful of people including Ingrid and Huxley—they were standing up for them—and Brenda, who smiled and dabbed her eyes as they arrived in front of the justice of the peace. Brenda had been pulling double duty as both mother of the bride and groom. Very soon, Melodie thought with secretive joy, she would also play honorary grandmother.

"Why don't we start trying?" Roman had said one night soon after they'd set a date.

They hadn't rushed their wedding plans, partly to give themselves time. He hadn't cracked open like an egg the moment they'd become engaged, and it had often been a two-steps-forward-one-step-back process. "Can we talk about it later?" was one of his favorite responses, but he rarely made her wait more than a day or two before he found whatever words he needed to explain his thoughts or feelings.

A baby was a huge decision, though. "Are you sure?" she'd asked, so anxious to start a family she could hardly function, but it had to be right for both of them or it could set them back. She knew that.

"It's all I think about," he'd admitted sheepishly. "I've been thinking about it since we got engaged. I'm more than sure. I'm impatient."

She'd laughed and they'd tried.

And earlier she'd done more than put on a gown in the short hour of privacy he'd given her. She'd taken a test. She was bursting with anticipation, eager to give him their wedding gift.

But she had to say her vows first. He knew something was up. They read each other very well these days, and his gaze sharpened, delving into hers, smiling at how widely she was grinning as they exchanged rings and clasped hands, binding themselves together with more than promises and a piece of paper. More than a new life even.

Love bound them, the kind of eternal connection that no one could put asunder.

"I do," she said when it was time. Then "I love you," hearing it back again in his sure timbre, just before they kissed. And when her lips were against his ear, she whispered, "We're having a baby."

She felt the shock go through him. He drew back and cupped her face. His expression was awed and dumbfounded, easily interpreted as he tried to assimilate this information while a huge beam of pride and excitement lit his face, no reservations and nothing held back. He shook his head, bemused and pleased. "I thought we were celebrating how happy we've been so far, but there's lots more to come after today, isn't there?"

"You're starting to sound like an optimist," she teased.

"That was confidence, sweetheart. I don't hope. I know." He stopped her laugh with a kiss.

* * * * *

#3373 SEDUCING HIS ENEMY'S DAUGHTER
by Annie West

Donato Salazar's plan to jilt his enemy's daughter is the ultimate revenge and beautiful Ella Sanderson is certainly sweet enough! But as their fake wedding day approaches, one question weighs heavily on Donato's mind: to love, honor...and betray?

#3374 HIDDEN IN THE SHEIKH'S HAREM
by Michelle Conder

When Prince Zachim Darkhan escapes capture he takes the daughter of his nemesis with him. But while Farah Hajjar is hidden in his harem the line between hatred and desire soon blurs, leading Zachim past the point of no return.

#3375 THE RETURN OF ANTONIDES
by Anne McAllister

Widow Holly Halloran's fresh start is only a plane ride away, until Lukas Antonides—the man she wishes she could forget—strides arrogantly back into her life. As tension mounts between them, so too does that bubbling attraction of old...

#3376 RESISTING THE SICILIAN PLAYBOY
by Amanda Cinelli

Leo Valente is as notorious as the tabloids say he is. But feisty wedding planner Dara Devlin isn't deterred. She needs his family castle for her top client, so she boldly accepts Leo's outrageous challenge to be his fake girlfriend!

REQUEST YOUR
FREE BOOKS!

HARLEQUIN

Presents®

2 FREE NOVELS PLUS
2 FREE GIFTS!

PASSION GUARANTEED SEDUCTION

YES! Please send me 2 FREE Harlequin Presents® novels and my 2 FREE gifts (gifts are worth about $10). After receiving them, if I don't wish to receive any more books, I can return the shipping statement marked "cancel." If I don't cancel, I will receive 6 brand-new novels every month and be billed just $4.30 per book in the U.S. or $5.24 per book in Canada. That's a saving of at least 13% off the cover price! It's quite a bargain! Shipping and handling is just 50¢ per book in the U.S. and 75¢ per book in Canada.* I understand that accepting the 2 free books and gifts places me under no obligation to buy anything. I can always return a shipment and cancel at any time. Even if I never buy another book, the two free books and gifts are mine to keep forever.

106/306 HDN GHRP

Name _____ (PLEASE PRINT)

Address _____ Apt. #

City _____ State/Prov. _____ Zip/Postal Code

Signature (if under 18, a parent or guardian must sign)

Mail to the **Reader Service:**
IN U.S.A.: P.O. Box 1867, Buffalo, NY 14240-1867
IN CANADA: P.O. Box 609, Fort Erie, Ontario L2A 5X3

**Are you a current subscriber to Harlequin Presents® books
and want to receive the larger-print edition?
Call 1-800-873-8635 or visit www.ReaderService.com.**

* Terms and prices subject to change without notice. Prices do not include applicable taxes. Sales tax applicable in N.Y. Canadian residents will be charged applicable taxes. Offer not valid in Quebec. This offer is limited to one order per household. Not valid for current subscribers to Harlequin Presents books. All orders subject to credit approval. Credit or debit balances in a customer's account(s) may be offset by any other outstanding balance owed by or to the customer. Please allow 4 to 6 weeks for delivery. Offer available while quantities last.

HP15

"Are you asking me to pose as your date?"

"What other reason would we have for being in Palermo together? I think it's the most believable scenario, don't you?"

Maybe it was tiredness after the past twenty-four hours catching up with her, but Dara felt a wave of hysterical laughter threatening to bubble up to the surface. The thought that anyone would believe a man like Leo Valente was dating a plain Irish nobody like her was absolutely ludicrous.

He continued, oblivious to her stunned reaction. "You would leave the business talk to me. All I'd need is for you to act as a buffer of sorts—play on your history with his family. Someone with a personal connection to smooth the way."

"A buffer? That sounds so flattering…" she muttered.

"You would get all the benefits of being my companion, being a guest at an exclusive event. It would be enjoyable, I believe."

"Umberto Lucchesi is a powerful man. He must have good reason not to trust you," she mused. "I'm not quite sure I can risk my reputation."

"I'm a powerful man, Dara. You climbed up a building to get a meeting with me. I'm offering you an opportunity to get exactly what you want. It's up to you if you take it or not."

The limo came to a stop. Dara looked out at the hotel's dull gray exterior, trying desperately to get a handle on the situation. He was essentially offering her the *castello* on a silver platter. All she had to do was play a part until he got his meeting and she would be done.

"What happens if you're wrong? If having a buffer makes no difference?"

"Let me worry about that. My offer is simple. Come with me to Palermo and I will sign your event contract for the castle."

She thought about the risk of trusting him. He hadn't given her any reason to trust him so far. But what other possible reason could he have for asking her to go with him?

A man like him could have any woman he wanted, so it wasn't simply attraction—she was sure of that.

He obviously wanted in on the Lucchesi deal very badly if it had prompted him to consider her event. His reaction earlier had been a complete contrast, his refusal so clear. It was a risk to lie to a man like Umberto Lucchesi, but on the scale of things it was more of a white lie. And the alternative meant losing the contract. Losing everything she had worked for.

"If I go with you—" she said it quickly, before she could change her mind "—I want a contract for the *castello* up front."

Leo felt triumph course through him as he felt Dara's shift toward accepting his offer. He'd seen the uncertainty on her face, knew the difficult position he was placing her in.

"You don't trust me, Dara?"

"Not even a little bit."

Don't miss
RESISTING THE SICILIAN PLAYBOY
by Amanda Cinelli,
available October 2015 wherever
Harlequin Presents® books and ebooks are sold.

www.Harlequin.com